Ballet  Academy

Ballet Academy

A Question of Character

BEATRICE MASINI

Translation by Laura Watkinson

PICCADILLY PRESS • LONDON

First published in Great Britain in 2009
by Piccadilly Press Ltd,
5 Castle Road, London NW1 8PR
www.piccadillypress.co.uk

Text copyright © Beatrice Masini, 2005
English language translation © Laura Watkinson 2009
Translated from the original *Che Caratterino!*
published by Edizioni EL, Trieste, Italy
www.edizioniel.com
Published by arrangement with Rights People, London

The right of Beatrice Masini to be identified as Author
of this work has been asserted by her in accordance with
the Copyright, Designs and Patents Act, 1988.

A catalogue record for this book is available
from the British Library.

ISBN: 978 1 84812 030 3

Printed in the UK by CPI Bookmarque, Croydon CR0 4TD
Cover design by Patrick Knowles
Cover illustration by Sara Not

CHAPTER ONE

The Holidays

When she was away on holiday, Zoe always felt she was beyond time and space; as if she was suspended in mid-air – floating, free. It was partly because she could forget the usual rules and routines of Ballet Academy and partly because when she went to a different place, *she* felt different too. This year, she'd gone on holiday with her family to the French Alps for the whole month of August – a place they'd never visited before.

They had rented an apartment with a large balcony full of geraniums. The geraniums made such an effort to be red and luxuriant that they seemed to be in competition with the geraniums in the surrounding windowboxes. Zoe was sharing a room with Maria. Sara was the oldest, so she was allowed to have her own room, but it was fine – Zoe didn't mind sharing with her little sister.

From the small balcony of their room, Zoe could look out over the perfect green of the gently sloping meadow, and breathe in the grass-scented air, which smelled like an enormous cup of herbal tea. As she stood there, Zoe felt like a perfect stranger, a stranger even to herself somehow.

There were some other children staying in the ground-floor apartment, and others in the building next door, which was separated from theirs only by a low fence. As far as those new children were concerned, Zoe wasn't a ballerina from the prestigious Ballet Academy and she wasn't the girl that she normally was outside of school either. Instead, she was just a fun, wild girl, rather unpredictable and full of great ideas.

One day, though, she told Alice – her almost instant best friend – all about herself. It was raining and they'd holed up in the bedroom, both of them sitting on the top bunk where Zoe slept, with the sloping roof just above their heads. It felt like being up a tree or in a secret den. Strange, almost grey, light filtered through the lace curtains, and there was perfect silence outside.

'I'm studying dance,' Zoe said out of the blue.

Alice looked at her from beneath her thick blond fringe and replied, 'I play basketball. But I might stop in

September – I want to try out martial arts.'

Zoe could tell that Alice hadn't understood (how could she?), so she continued, 'It's really serious, though, what I'm doing.'

And then she told her all about the Academy, and Alice opened her eyes wide when she heard the name of the school, because even though she lived in a town by the sea, miles and miles away from Zoe, *everyone* had heard of the Ballet Academy.

Zoe told her about Madame Olenska, probably the strictest teacher in the world, and all about Leda and her other friends. She explained about the school rules and the really tough entrance procedure and end-of-year exams, and she told Alice about all of the children who started at the school and then had to leave because they couldn't cope. She told her how exciting the recitals were and about the hard work they had to do every day. Finally, the two girls sat in silence, just listening to the water gurgling in the gutter.

'Wow,' Alice said after quite a long time. 'I've never met a real ballerina before.'

'But I'm not a real ballerina yet,' Zoe said. 'I might be one day. I don't know for sure.'

'You're so lucky, knowing what you want to be when you grow up,' Alice said. 'I still haven't decided. Maybe an archaeologist or a vet. Hmm. Hey, I think it might have stopped raining.'

Zoe reached over to the window and pulled the curtain aside. Alice was right. The world outside was dripping wet, but it was calm, and the light was changing – it was more golden, more colourful. A moment later, they were outside, and that was the end of the conversation.

Later that evening, listening to the gentle breathing of her little sister in the bunk below, Zoe lay awake and wondered whether she *was* really certain about what she wanted to do when she grew up. Try as she might, she couldn't quite answer the question. Five minutes later, though, she was asleep, and she didn't think about it again for ages. It wasn't really the sort of thing she wanted to think about on holiday.

A few days later, all of Zoe's family went on a trip with Alice's family. Alice was one of three children too, but she had brothers and they were all older than her. They made quite a crowd. They'd set themselves a challenging walk to a mountain hut beside a small lake, which would take them about three hours, and was all uphill. After an hour and a half, Maria sat down on a rock and wailed that she couldn't take another step. Ed and Luke, Alice's brothers, were tired too but they obviously didn't want to admit it. It was Sara who finally convinced Maria to carry on by promising to give her one of her old dolls once they got home. And so the walk continued. Zoe was the only one who never stopped and never complained. It really didn't feel like much of an effort to her.

'Of course it's easy for you. You're a ballerina!' Alice panted at her when they finally reached their goal and collapsed on the benches outside the mountain hut.

Zoe just smiled. There were advantages to being a ballerina: her body was used to doing what she told it to – it obeyed instinctively, without being bullied into it.

Zoe opened up her rucksack, took out a bar of hazel-nut chocolate and broke it in half with a snap. 'Here you go,' she said to Alice, giving her one of the pieces. Zoe sank her teeth into the hard, crunchy chocolate and the delicious flavour filled her mouth. She felt proud of her body – proud and grateful too. It felt as though she was thanking her body by giving it this small pleasure.

When their holiday was over, Zoe and Alice swapped phone numbers and kept in touch by texting. Zoe's mum and dad had given her a mobile phone as a present at the end of the school year. It was so difficult to say anything important in just a few words, though. Texts were better for quick messages and jokes. Zoe started texting away like mad with Leda, her best friend. Leda hadn't been an instant best friend like Alice, but she'd been her best friend since forever – her real best friend.

Zoe and Leda met up quite often in the ten days before school started again, and Zoe told Leda all about Alice, but tried not to make their friendship sound too important. Leda had gone to the seaside for a fortnight with her dad (who had split up from her mum) and Leda had spent the entire time practically glued to him, because she was so happy to be with him. That meant she hadn't made any new friends or done anything much. But she was happy to keep talking about her dad, telling Zoe how her dad did this and her dad did that, and then he said this, and then he did that, and then he bought her a . . .

Zoe felt really sorry for Leda. She could see how much she missed her dad, but now that everything was returning back to normal, Leda would only see him once a week, twice if she was lucky.

A few days before school started again, Zoe realised she was almost happy that the holidays were nearly over. Going back to the Academy gave her a sense of security: knowing exactly what each day would be like and what she was going to be doing put her in a good mood.

It was an important September for Maria as well, because she was starting at a new school. She was pretending that it was no big deal, but every now and then a casual question slipped out and gave her away. 'What if the teacher doesn't like me?' Maria would ask suddenly, or 'What if I don't like the teacher?' A few nights before, when Zoe was almost asleep, she'd felt a warm little bundle snuggling up to her. 'Can I come into your bed?' It was Maria, sounding agitated.

'Of course,' said Zoe, and she wriggled over to make space for her sister. She stroked her hair to calm her down.

'I don't think I want to go to school,' Maria said after a while.

'Oh yes, you do,' Zoe told her. 'It's just that you don't know it. There's no way you can know how much fun it will be yet. You'll see.'

Then she reminded her of the things that you do at school – about new schoolbooks, reading, drawing, games . . . She made it sound as exciting as she could. And, after a while, Maria dropped off and all her little worries vanished into sleep. Zoe hugged her tight and thought how happy she was to have a sister who still needed her sometimes.

CHAPTER TWO

New Arrivals

Zoe may have been looking forward to the comforting familiarity of a new school year, but there were always a few surprises too. One of the things Zoe had to do back at school was go to the costume department, to try on her new leotard. Now that she was one of the first year seniors, she'd left behind the simple, sleeveless leotard that the juniors wore. The uniform was still black, but with three-quarter-length sleeves and a beautiful short skirt.

Demetra, the head of the costume department, saw Zoe coming in and immediately said, 'Have you seen how gorgeous the new teacher is?'

Zoe was amazed, mostly at hearing Demetra talking

about a teacher like that, but also because she hadn't known that there was going to be a new teacher. When she went to the changing rooms to get ready for the first lesson, the news was spreading fast.

'His name's Kai Zwerger,' Paula announced. Paula always knew everything about everybody. 'He's studied in Paris and New York.'

'He's twenty-eight,' added Francine, wrinkling her nose. 'A bit too old for me.'

'Yes, but have you seen his beautiful eyes?' Paula said. 'They're so yummy I could almost eat them up.'

Zoe couldn't help grinning as she imagined Paula the cannibal using a dainty silver fork to spear two blue eyes – his eyes would just have to be blue, wouldn't they – and then popping them into her mouth like a couple of grapes or cherry tomatoes.

'What are you smiling at, Zoe?' said Paula, who never missed anything.

'Oh, nothing. I was just thinking,' Zoe answered. 'Who were you talking about?'

'The new teacher for character dance,' they all chorused.

Zoe didn't say anything, she just drifted into a day-dream. Zoe really, really loved character dance – the rich variety of folk dances that found their way into classical ballet. Some of the tunes seemed to beat in Zoe's muscles, and pulse around her body with her blood. And when that happened she just let herself go and let the rhythm carry her along.

Their lessons also included trying out more interpretative styles of dance, which Zoe loved too, because her body was so free to move, and so was her face. She didn't need to have that fixed smile on her lips that made ballerinas look like dolls. She could scowl or grimace. Even her fingers and toes played a part and weren't imprisoned by the classical positions. And her shoulders and neck got to join in too – the whole body was used, so Zoe could transform herself into a cat, a bear, a frog . . . the only limit was her imagination.

'Hey, Zoe. Are you ready?' Leda startled Zoe out of her trance and brought her back down to earth. 'Come on! The lesson's starting.'

And then they were at the barre, each of them chained to the spot by Madame Olenska's fierce and forceful gaze.

At the beginning of the class, she said, 'Good morning and best wishes for the new school year. The first year of senior school will be very, very demanding. To those of you who have already studied with me, I will only say that you will have to work even harder than before.' And she ran her eyes over last year's students: Anna and Francine, Laila, Leda and Zoe, Paula, Sophie, Estelle, Stephanie, Alissa on one side, and Lucas, Roberto, Matthew and Jamie at the back.

'As for the new arrivals,' she continued, 'I can only hope that you have talent and dedication. Without talent, dedication is useless. But without dedication, talent just withers and dies, like a flower without water. Just like this.' She used her hands to mime a flower wilting away.

Zoe couldn't resist the temptation to peek in the mirror to see the expressions of the two new students. There was Haydée, whose incredibly red hair went all the way down to her waist when she let it loose – although at the moment, of course, she had it up in a big, full bun for the lesson. And there was Leo, who had very dark eyes hiding beneath a fringe that was just a bit too long. Haydée looked nervous, but Leo seemed calm. Zoe would almost have thought he was smiling, if it weren't for the fact that smiling was not acceptable in lessons, unless Madame Olenska instructed you to do so. Both new students had already introduced themselves to the class during normal lessons. They seemed nice, but it was hard to tell anything more at this early stage.

Then the lesson began, and everything was the same as usual, or so it seemed to Zoe. She didn't feel another year older. She didn't even think she'd grown all that much. She was wearing the shoes that she'd bought for the end-of-year recital and her exam. That all seemed like such a long time ago although it was only ten weeks before – something that somebody else had done. Zoe could remember all of the exercises that Madame had ordered her to do for the exam, one after the other, watched by the critical eyes of the committee. She'd danced very calmly, almost clinically. But everything had gone fine, which must mean that emotion wasn't a required ingredient.

However, now that she was thinking about character dance, Zoe felt a kind of excitement that was new to her. She wished they were in the other dance studio, up on the top floor. It had a view out over the city, so her imagination could really take off – and start to wander a long way, and become lost amongst the patterns of the roofs, the television aerials and the church spires. Of course, she really shouldn't spend all her time gazing out of the windows when a new teacher had come all the way from the other side of the world especially to teach her class how to do the kind of dancing that Zoe liked best.

'And three, and four.' Madame Olenska stopped beside Zoe. 'Zoe, are you still on holiday? Let me take this opportunity to remind you that the new school year has begun.'

It was strange, but Madame didn't seem quite as strict as usual. She almost seemed to be joking with Zoe so her words didn't make Zoe feel bad, but bounced off her skin like raindrops instead. *Fine then, I'll concentrate,* Zoe thought, and she really did. She banished her wandering thoughts and concentrated fully on the barre, the wooden floor and the gentle motion of legs bending and straightening, up and down, up and down.

* * *

Afterwards in the changing room, Leda, who had already changed, flopped down on the bench beside Zoe, as limp as an empty sack.

'The first days back are such hard work!' she puffed.

Zoe didn't answer her, but just carried on unlacing her ballet shoes, very, very slowly. She let the ribbons fall, then picked them up and laced her shoes again.

'What are you doing, Zoe? Everyone's going home, the lessons are over, o-o-over,' Leda pronounced very clearly, waving a hand in front of Zoe's face. 'You're acting really weirdly today. You've got your head in the clouds. You're not in love, are you?'

'Who with?' Zoe laughed, because the idea seemed so silly.

Sara, though – she *was* in love! Zoe's big fourteen-year-old sister had finally started dating a boy who had been after her forever, not without a little encouragement from Zoe. Now it was Stephen this, Stephen that, Stephen the other whenever Sara was around. There was no way Zoe would ever talk like that about a boy, even if she happened to like him and especially not if she were actually going out with him. But Leda wasn't going to let the subject drop.

'Maybe it's Leo,' giggled Leda. Zoe stared at Leda in amazement. Leda knew her really well, so why was she teasing Zoe in the kind of annoying way that Paula would?

'Leo? Do you think I could fall in love with someone with a name like that?' Zoe replied coolly.

'It's a very artistic name, actually,' said Leda, in a very serious voice. 'And anyway, he's so handsome! Alissa's already invited him over to hers. She said they could do their homework together. Ha! You should've seen her, the silly girl.'

Zoe was surprised at the way Leda was talking, but she tried not to let it show. Leda was normally so reserved, so cautious, and so kind to everyone. 'If anyone's acting weirdly, it's you,' she wanted to say. The words were there, ready, on the tip of her tongue, but then they vanished.

They walked home together, as they had done so many times before, and as they would way into the future. September was a beautiful month in the city – warm, but nice and fresh at the same time, and the days were still long, although night came suddenly, like a curtain falling. They didn't talk on the bus, because it was too loud. They would have had to shout and Zoe didn't feel like it and neither, it seemed, did Leda.

When Zoe got off the bus, they waved goodbye to each other frantically, one of them from the pavement and the other from behind the glass of the bus window, as though they wouldn't be seeing each other for a long time. Zoe thought about it: she spent more time with Leda than she did with her mum or dad, or her sisters. Leda was like a member of the family. So why did she feel so distant from her since they'd returned to school?

Maybe it's me, maybe it's my fault, she finally thought to herself. She felt very mixed up inside. But then, being distant from her long-standing best friend would have that effect, Zoe thought. Not to mention Madame Olenska's little speech that afternoon, which had been buzzing around Zoe's head ever since: talent and dedication, dedication and talent.

Alone in her room later, with the door closed and her elbows resting on the windowsill, she wondered if she had those two gifts – dedication and talent. Did she have one more than the other? And which one was more important? Zoe wondered if growing up just meant asking a lot of questions that she didn't have the answers to.

Suddenly Maria threw open Zoe's bedroom door (without knocking, as usual), ran in and leaped on Zoe, like a little monkey.

All in one breath Maria said, 'Did you know, I started my new school today. And you know what? You were right! It was really great.' And that was the end of Zoe's quiet moment.

It turned out that Kai Zwerger's eyes really were blue. More than that, their shade of deep blue seemed to hold a kind of magic spell that made everything they rested upon more beautiful, more enchanting. They were the kind of eyes that made Zoe want to be good and look perfect, in the hope that they would rest their magic glow upon her. Zoe wondered what Kai's eyes looked like when he was angry. Maybe they were like a thunderstorm that left the watcher breathless at its power. But Kai wasn't likely to get angry and he obviously wouldn't want to scare anybody at this early stage. What he really would want was to gain their trust.

He spoke English well, with a foreign accent that you could hardly hear, but sometimes he slowed down and was clearly trying to find the right word. He was very precise. A dance teacher had to be precise.

Today they were in the room with the beautiful view, but there could have been a wonderful rainbow outside or the most spectacular sunset of the year or even a whirlwind and no one would have noticed. They were all listening in perfect silence and every eye in the room was focused on Kai.

'I have a passion for character dance,' he was saying. 'I know that it's considered a bit of a poor relation to classical ballet and contemporary dance; the Cinderella of the dance world, if you like. But even Cinderella became a princess, didn't she?'

Lots of heads nodded.

'I believe in character dance, because I firmly believe that dance is all about expressing emotion. And in character dance it's easier to find a way of doing that. However, note that I didn't say it was easy. To express emotions, you need to actually feel them. Faking it isn't good enough. If you pretend, you're just a puppet. You need to be an actor.'

Zoe felt a shiver run down her spine – she knew exactly what he meant. Being an actor didn't mean pretending, but something else. Feeling the emotion, and using it.

'I haven't yet decided what the course programme will be. We'll improvise, like actors do. And then we'll try to choose the right path together. Okay?'

Lots of heads were nodding again. They knew that the best part was coming. They were right.

'Well, I think that's enough talking. I have nothing else to say and we have so much to do. I suggest a simple exercise, so that we can get to know each other. I'll start the music now and we'll listen to it all the way through. Really listen to the music. I want you to feel what it's telling you. Then, one by one, you're going to dance across the room. However you like, with whatever steps you want to use. Okay? Here we go then.'

Click. The CD started. Zoe was certain that she'd heard the music somewhere before – maybe her dad had listened to it at home. It was in a minor key, but it wasn't sad, but rather solemn and full of dignity like a fierce ache, a proud pain. No, that was too difficult – how could you dance an ache? Maybe it would be better to think of something simpler. An animal. What animal was this music? A big animal, a powerful one, but one that was light on its feet. A ferocious one? Yes. A big one. A fast one. A lion, that was it! A lion. Suddenly the music finished. Kai (it felt wrong to use his surname) bent over the CD player and pressed the button again.

'First the boys,' he said.

Lucas went first. He did what he was best at doing – he jumped. His leaps were beautiful, almost perfect. Maybe too perfect, thought Zoe.

This music was more about imprecise jumps, improvised, unplanned moves. And now she was really hoping that no one who danced before her would have thought of a lion, because the lion was hers, and it was already prowling around inside her head and getting ready to pounce. The other boys were doing jumps as well. They were copying Lucas, certain that whatever he'd done would be right – even Leo, the new boy.

Laila, however, went for a series of pirouettes. They were very tight pirouettes, danced on *demi-pointe*, with a long slide separating them whenever the music called for it. She was very good, as always, but, to be honest, Zoe thought, a little dull. Then some of the other girls had their turns. Then, finally, it was Zoe's turn. Luckily for her, the music was just starting from the beginning again. The start of the music was the part that she liked best. And the lion jumped! It leaped and then crouched, as if resting briefly while it considered its prey. Another jump, another crouch; a jump, head back, arms too; and down, the head pressed to the knees, as though to gather energy. This was a lion limbering up for the hunt and really enjoying himself. Zoe's lion liked the preparation almost as much as the hunt itself.

It was a pity that the diagonal path across the room was so short, even in that huge room beneath the roof. It was already over, and the lion still had a lot of jumps left in his muscles. Never mind. Zoe landed for the last time, crouched into a ball, and then stood up and slid over to the wall. She leaned her back against the barre, in a resting position, and watched as the others invented their own series of moves. Alissa came up with the idea of an animal too. You could tell immediately that it was a deer or something like that. But all of the other girls went through a series of classical steps, just a slightly simplified version. Leda, who was the last one, used more contemporary ballet steps, which meant long, languid movements, which was what she did best.

Kai waited for the music to finish and then pressed a button on the CD player. 'Well done,' he said. 'I felt some of you were trying to tell me something. Others decided to show me how good they are. I don't want you to be good when you're with me. I want you to be yourselves. That's the only way you *can* be really good. I'm not sure I've made myself clear. Perhaps it'll be a bit difficult to start with, but I'd like to show you what I hear within this music, and how

I let it communicate through my body.'

He turned the CD player on again. The music started. What moved through the room, not just along the diagonal path, but throughout the entire space, was not an animal – it wasn't even a human being, it seemed more like a half-man, half-animal something, with a horse below and a man on top Zoe thought. What kind of creature was that? Grace, muscle, power . . . it came to her in a flash: a centaur. A mythical being charging through a forest, following its natural instincts. Of course, it was beautiful to watch. Kai was an expert, after all. He was a teacher. But Zoe knew that it was more than that – it was because he was so entirely absorbed in what he was doing.

'He's really great, isn't he?' said Lucas as they were walking down the steps after school.

'Oh, yes,' agreed Zoe.

'I don't know whether I really understood what it was that he wanted from us, but I still think he's great,' he continued. And then he gave Zoe a bit of a funny look. 'I think you were the best,' he said. 'After him, of course,' and he gave her a lopsided grin.

'Thanks,' said Zoe. 'That's kind of you.'

'No, it isn't,' said Lucas. 'I'm just saying what I think is true. See you tomorrow.' And he dashed off to catch up with Matthew.

Leda wasn't around – her dad had come to pick her up so they could go out for a pizza together. She'd been fizzing with excitement about it, getting changed after class quick as a flash, and heading straight out with her bun still up. Zoe thought Leda looked a bit strange with her bright-pink hooded top with a big sequinned flower on the front, baggy jeans, trainers deliberately left undone, and then that neat and tidy bun on top of her head. It looked like she was two people in one.

That evening, at home, Zoe found her dad reading the paper. She crept up below it and poked her head up in front of the page he was reading, her face twinkling up at him from underneath the day's headlines. Her dad looked down at her questioningly; he was used to this manoeuvre.

'Let's play a game,' Zoe suggested. 'I'll hum a tune and you have to tell me what it is.'

'What do I get if I win?' her dad asked, putting the paper down and smiling.

'A kiss?'

'Make it three and you've got a deal.'

Zoe hummed Kai's tune. Her dad had a glint in his eye straightaway, but he let her finish. Zoe quite wanted to hum the whole thing anyway, but especially the first section, the part she'd danced that afternoon.

'It's Beethoven,' he told her when she'd finished. 'The Allegretto from the Seventh Symphony.'

'Could you play it for me?'

'Of course,' her dad said.

He stood up and looked through the neatly ordered CDs. They filled half of the shelves; the other half was taken up by her mum's books.

'Here it is,' he said, putting the CD into the player.

A moment later, the music was rising up out of the speakers, full and rich and intense. Zoe's fingers and toes were tingling – she wanted to dance as she had that afternoon, but she felt a bit too shy, so she just listened.

'It's beautiful,' her dad commented when the music had finished.

'I danced to that music today,' Zoe said.

It felt as though she was revealing a secret. Her dad seemed to understand perfectly. He didn't say anything, but just looked at her with so much affection in his eyes that it felt almost as though he was giving her a hug.

Then, after a while, he said, 'How about my kisses then?' and Zoe smiled and jumped on to his lap.

Mum found the two of them like that. 'Have you two quite finished with all that cuddling? Your dinner's ready, if I'm not disturbing you.' And she gave the two of them a smile – a smile that felt like another hug.

CHAPTER THREE

Girls

Kai was extraordinary, he had beautiful eyes and his classes were really exciting, but they only had him twice a week. That wasn't anything like often enough and it didn't make up for everything else – the usual school stuff and Madame Olenska's awful lessons, which seemed to be focused on the arms, shoulders, head and neck this year.

It wasn't as though Madame had stopped paying attention to their feet, though. When a *plié* was too sloppy, or a *battement tendu* was not sufficiently *tendu*, or stretched, she banged her cane insistently on the floor, making everyone jump, while the guilty party withered away beneath her merciless gaze. It may well be illegal to use the cane to hit pupils nowadays, but the sharp noise was quite enough.

Laila was the calmest of all of them in Madame Olenska's classes. Laila had a natural gift: her head was perched atop a long and agile neck and her shoulders sloped elegantly, in the same slightly old-fashioned look that you saw in portraits of nineteenth-century ballerinas like Marie Taglioni and Fanny Elssler, the great rivals. Reproductions of their portraits hung in the corridor that led from the classrooms to the dance studios.

When Zoe was small, the portraits were too high for her to see properly, so they'd all looked identical, but she'd learned to tell them apart and she sometimes used to stop to look at them and try to guess their secrets. But all she could see were ringlets, pretty faces with mysterious and distant smiles, and unusually long tutus that did more to conceal the legs than show them off.

One of Zoe's teachers had told her that Marie Taglioni had an exceptionally good teacher – her own father. Zoe thought it would be horrible to have your dad as your teacher, always ready to yell at you, to tell you off, always focused on his work: you.

Anyway Laila, who looked like one of those old-fashioned ballerinas already, really didn't have to make any effort to be the best. But outside dancing, she remained isolated and withdrawn. She was a girl of very few words – and the few words she said were usually mean.

The other day she'd said to Paula, 'Please, go right on thinking and talking about boys all the time. With any luck, they'll throw you out.'

Laila had grinned horribly as she'd said it. It was the kind of grin that made Zoe itch to wipe it off her face with a good slap. When she felt that aggressive (it was that prowling lion again), Zoe almost frightened herself. What if her fists really did run away with her one day? The school might suspend her for something like that. But in any case, Laila's grin hadn't lasted long. Paula had snapped right back.

'Well, at least I'm thinking about boys because they think about me. There's no way anyone would want to think about you, is there?'

And it was true that the boys weren't interested in Laila, with her doll-like face and her posing and her attitude. They were, however, interested in Paula. Paula wore make-up, even though the students weren't supposed to, and her breasts had started to grow. The tight black leotard flattened her chest, but the soft, skimpy tops she usually wore showed off her new figure very well. All of the boys looked at Paula. Zoe wasn't sure how she felt about that. She didn't have anything for the boys to look at yet and she wasn't even sure that she wanted them to look at her, but Zoe wondered if she might change her mind, depending on who was looking.

* * *

In fact, it was all so confusing that on Saturday morning (Bliss! No school!) she slipped into Sara's room for a chat. Sara was still in bed, but she wasn't asleep – she was listening to loud music and painting her nails purple.

In the gap between one thump of music and the next, Zoe asked her, straight out, 'Do you think that anyone could ever fancy me?'

Sara looked up from painting the nail on her little finger, which was a perfect purple almond shape, dark and shiny. She blew on her nail, looked at Zoe, and said, 'That's quite a serious question, isn't it? Come and sit over here with me.'

Zoe went over and curled up on the bed next to Sara, a bit nervously, since Sara's opinion on this subject counted for quite a lot.

Sara looked into her eyes and said, 'Zoe you're really, really pretty. And I'm not just saying that because you're my sister. I'm saying it because it's what I think. Your body's fantastic. Your legs are a mile long, you've got beautiful hair with natural highlights, expressive eyes . . .' She carried on listing Zoe's good points. 'With those eyelashes you don't even need mascara. Mine look like a worn-out old brush in comparison.'

Sara fluttered her eyelashes at Zoe to demonstrate, but it wasn't very convincing, because even without make-up (and she'd started wearing make-up every day now), Sara was absolutely stunning.

'But,' she continued, tilting her head to consider Zoe from different angles, studying her as if she were some kind of strange, new species, 'maybe you could make yourself look a bit more interesting. I don't know . . . I mean, look at that sweatshirt. It looks like a sack. And your jeans, who designed them? Turn around, so I can take a look. No, never heard of them. You know, if you wear designer stuff, it makes you feel more confident,' she said, as though she were revealing some great secret. 'It's not as though they necessarily look better. It's just that they make you feel right, so you're more comfortable. And if you feel comfortable, you're more attractive.'

It was a strange theory, and Zoe tried hard to understand it. The smell of the nail varnish was making her feel a bit dazed.

'But how do you make yourself more interesting?' she asked Sara.

'Ah. That's the most difficult thing. You have to be mysterious, create the impression that you have a secret, that kind of thing.'

'Could you give me another example?' Zoe still didn't understand.

'No, I can't. It's just something that you have to feel. Either you get it, or you don't.'

'And I suppose you get it, don't you?' said Zoe, a bit grumpily.

If there was no proper explanation, if there was no method as such, what was Zoe supposed to do? If she didn't understand a dance exercise at school, she stayed behind after class and went into an empty practice room and, in front of the mirror, repeated the exercise dozens of times, even hundreds, and did the same the next day, and the next day, until she'd perfected it. It might be tiring, it might be torture, but it was the only way.

'Well, yes, kind of,' said Sara. 'You'll get it too if you think it's worth bothering about. But if you want to be interesting, that means you must be interested in someone, doesn't it? So, are you going to tell me who it is?'

Right at that moment, someone knocked on the door and then opened it without waiting for an answer. It was Mum. 'Oops, were you two having a private chat?' she said, with a smile in her voice.

'Muuum,' grumbled Sara. 'We were talking about a very serious matter.'

'I'm sure you were,' said their mum. 'But we've got plans for this morning. Remember? Now get a move on!' And she pulled Sara's duvet off the bed.

'Oh yes, we're going round to Gran's for brunch, aren't we? She might make pancakes for us,' said Sara, her eyes gleaming.

Zoe looked at her. Suddenly her big, streetwise sister had disappeared and there was just a girl almost like her, with a face bare of make-up and bright blue eyes that gleamed with pleasure at the thought of something as simple as Gran's pancakes.

'I'm sure she will,' said their mum. 'She only ever makes pancakes when it's the wrong time of year for pancakes, doesn't she?'

Maybe *that's* what it's all about, thought Zoe. Doing unpredictable things. That's what you have to do if you want to be interesting.

It turned out that Haydée was very interesting. She had an American mum and a French name. Her dad was the head of a big multinational company with offices all over the world, so she'd lived in six different cities since she was born. She'd even lived in Kinshasa, in Africa, which, as she had said when she was telling them her life story, is the capital of the Democratic Republic of the Congo.

'Obviously I didn't study dance there,' she laughed.

She had very small teeth, like pearls. Haydée could speak four languages, and when she grew up she wanted to be a diplomat so that she could see all the parts of the world that she hadn't seen yet.

'What about being a ballerina?' Sophie asked her.

'What do you mean?'

'Don't you want to be a ballerina?'

Zoe could tell she really meant: If not, what are you doing here?

'Oh, I don't know,' Haydée said, tossing her head back

with a rippling cascade of red hair. 'It's a bit early to decide, isn't it? A million things could happen, couldn't they?' And then, with a dramatic change of subject, she said, 'Do you know how to play dodgeball?'

The unanimous answer was no, but when she explained the rules they found that it was quite similar to one of their usual games, but with just a few tiny changes. It had sounded far more exciting when Haydée called it dodgeball, but they found out that Haydée was a disaster at the game. Zoe wondered why Haydée had suggested it, since she seemed to drop the ball more than anyone else, or just threw it too hard. Zoe also noticed that every time Haydée made a mistake, she laughed and shook her hair, again and again.

Zoe wasn't sure she particularly liked Haydée after the dodgeball, and when Roberto started staring at Haydée in a way that made a little knot form in Zoe's stomach, Zoe suddenly found out a few things at once:

1) She, Zoe, was interested in Roberto (who was she kidding? That wasn't a surprise);

2) Roberto was probably not interested in her;

3) There are people who manage to make themselves interesting by doing the exact opposite of what might be thought interesting, and

4) There are people who are naturally interesting without having to make any effort at all.

For Zoe, being interesting seemed like it was going to

be really hard work. She had played really well, as she usually did, and showed that she'd grasped the differences between dodgeball their usual game really quickly. She helped her team, which was also Roberto's team, to win, but he didn't even glance at her during the entire game, or afterwards in English class, or even after that in Kai's character dance lesson.

At least they'd had a really good interpretative session. The gentle autumn light illuminated the beautiful room beneath the roof, as Saint-Saëns' *Carnival of the Animals* surged from the speakers and their teacher acted out the animals in turn: swans and lions and donkeys and elephants and penguins. It was a wild and crazy zoo. It was actually really hilarious, but, fortunately, Kai was the sort of teacher you could have a laugh with. He really made you want to join in, to challenge him and find new ways to mimic the same animal. Laila did a really good penguin. Leda, of course, was a swan, but her swan was a dramatic one, not a soppy, dying one like in *Swan Lake*. Estelle even managed to imitate the difficult concept of an echo, using her body and her arms to show the sound waves.

It was such good fun. As they finished, they were all chattering away excitedly. For once, it wasn't the usual competition to see who was the best, because they were all pretty good in their own way, doing their own thing. If only it were always that easy for them to get on together.

'Okay, ladies and gentlemen, I'll see you on Thursday,' Kai said as they left the room. 'I'm really happy with the way you're working, but I expect you to be this good all the time, if not better. Bring your thinking caps with you when you come to class. We could all benefit from some new ideas.'

'Did you hear that?' Leda said, as they were getting changed. 'He didn't call us children! He called us ladies and gentlemen.'

CHAPTER FOUR

Affairs of the Heart

'Have you seen them?' Leda was whispering right into Zoe's ear, so it almost felt to Zoe as though she was yelling.

Zoe jumped and pulled away from Leda giving her a look of irritation. 'What on earth are you doing?' Zoe snapped, in a tone that she almost didn't recognise herself.

'I was just telling you. Anna and Jamie. Look at them. Over there in the corner. No, not now, or they'll see you looking. Pretend you haven't seen them. They're kissing. They're kissing!'

Zoe didn't want to turn around, but she did anyway, very slowly. It felt as though she were being attracted by a magnet. And she saw that Leda was right. Over in the corner, in the shelter of the tree, which really didn't seem like the most private of places, Jamie was giving Anna a kiss. On the cheek. Like a brother might. Only he wasn't her brother and, even worse, they were holding hands. Zoe turned away, quickly. She was a bit ashamed for having let her curiosity get the better of her.

'It's their business, isn't it? Let's just leave them to it,' she said to Leda. She felt as though she was being nosy and spying on them, taking a peep at a moment that didn't belong to her or to Leda or to anybody else who felt like watching.

'I wonder if they've kissed each other on the lips,' giggled Leda, a bit dreamily. 'I wonder what that's like. It must be complicated – your nose would get in the way, wouldn't it? What are you supposed to do with your nose when you kiss?'

Zoe didn't know what to say. It wasn't something that she'd ever wondered about herself, but it seemed like a pretty good question, so she couldn't help thinking about it.

'It's not a show that they're putting on for our benefit, you know,' she said to Leda, voicing her earlier thought.

'What's that got to do with noses?' Leda exclaimed. 'You know, I really don't understand you. You're always so serious. You're just no fun any more. I can't talk to you about anything.'

With a shrug of her shoulders, she strode off on her model-long legs to join Paula, Estelle and Stephanie, who, judging from the giggles and the way their heads were moving, were also commenting on the same scene. Zoe was left alone.

She'd been feeling lonely quite often lately, but she knew that there was a solution to that problem. She went up the stairs into the building and headed up to the first floor. She knocked at a door with frosted glass windows.

'Come in,' said a familiar voice, which was a bit low and hoarse.

In the costume department there was always a lovely smell of new fabrics and starch, because costume-makers didn't trust anyone else to iron the beautiful garments they spent so long creating. Demetra was ironing a costume with a really long violet tutu. The bodice was on the ironing board and the skirt was falling softly down at the sides. A ribbon in a paler shade of violet ran around the edge of the bodice and tied at the front in a bow. The bow was undone and Demetra was pressing down hard on the hem, trying to straighten it out.

She glanced up from her work and said, 'Oh, it's you, Zoe. How nice to see you.' Then she went back to pressing down on the hem, backwards and forwards, backwards and forwards.

'Who's that for?' Zoe breathed. 'It's beautiful.'

'Thank you, Zoe, I'm pleased with it. It's for Mariah

Simone to wear in the Gala of the Stars,' Demetra replied.

At least twice a year, the Academy Theatre hosted a pageant of stars from all over the world. They didn't perform an actual ballet, but a sort of anthology of the best things they'd done recently; soloists, *pas de deux* and short pieces specially choreographed by Jasper Jones, the director of the *corps de ballet*. Mariah Simone, the theatre's star ballerina, always had a solo spot. Mariah was like a role model for all of the children at the ballet school, because she had attended the school herself when she was a little girl, just like them, and, after she'd done all of her exams and gained her diploma, four world-class theatres wanted to have her, but she decided to stay where she was.

They sometimes saw Mariah walking down the school corridors, so they knew what she looked like from really close up and they could even have touched her, but no one ever dared. They just squeezed up close to the wall and waited for her to brush past, dazzled by her presence, by her gentle smile and by her steps, which were both light and precise.

This year, as everyone knew, she was going to dance a new piece by Jasper Jones called *Noblesse*, all on her own, because she was good enough to fill the stage all by herself.

'I didn't think she'd be wearing such a classic tutu,' said Zoe, curiously. 'I thought that Mr Jones would have created a modern piece for her.'

'It actually is a modern piece,' said Demetra. 'I had a peek at the rehearsals the other day. Can you imagine? Performing those peculiar movements while she's dressed in a classic tutu? It'll be quite something.'

Demetra wasn't very keen on contemporary dance, because she felt that it put her out of a job. One time when she was feeling particularly annoyed about it, she'd explained the problem to Zoe.

'They're either naked, or they're wearing a flesh-coloured leotard that makes it look as though they're naked, or they've got one of those skin-tight costumes that you can't do anything creative with. They're just like swimming costumes. So what do they need me for, eh?'

However, it seemed that on this occasion a compromise had been reached. The tutu was absolutely beautiful.

'Are you okay?' Demetra asked. 'Perhaps it's just the light in here, but you look a bit pale.'

'Demetra, I wanted to ask you something . . .' Zoe started, hesitantly.

'What is it, sweetheart?'

'In your opinion . . . how important is love?'

'What a question! That really is a million-dollar question. Why are you asking me about that? Are *you* in love?' And she peered at Zoe over the top of her half-moon glasses.

'I don't really know. But it's not about me. I just mean in general.'

'Oh, well, in that case . . . I think there's only one thing I know for sure: that love has many faces. There's all that business with your heart, when you really like someone, and you want to spend all of your time with them, and that's really, really important, maybe the most important thing of all. But not everyone is lucky enough to find the right person. And sometimes they find the right person, but then they lose them. So you have to make the effort to find love in lots of other places too, so that you never end up without love.'

Zoe wasn't sure what Demetra meant by finding love in different places, but she didn't want to seem stupid. Fortunately, Demetra seemed to hear her thoughts.

She continued, 'A mother has lots of love inside her: the love that she gives to her children and the love that they give to her, and that doesn't just stop when they've grown up and left home like my son William. And then in the rest of your life, you can either do things with love or you can do them without love, and there's a huge difference. A tutu made with love is different from one that was made grudgingly. Look at how that one there turned out . . .' And she nodded in the direction of a pink tutu hanging nearby.

It was a very classic style, with a ring of net sticking out horizontally around a velvet bodice with elaborate silver braid on it in a zigzag pattern. Zoe thought it was beautiful and said so. But Demetra was adamant that it was bad work and looked at the costume as though she wanted to set fire to it.

'But, Zoe, can't you see how stiff it is? It almost looks like it's frozen. And do you know why it turned out like that? Because it's for that nasty piece of work, Julia Monda, that's why. She swans in and out, never says hello, and thinks she's the bee's knees, but she's completely eaten up with jealousy for Mariah Simone. I swear, if she could get away with it, she'd quite happily break Mariah's leg.' As she spoke, Demetra waved the iron around like a weapon and pressed it against an imaginary Julia Monda.

Zoe laughed, and Demetra joined in. 'Yes, I think laughter's probably the best reaction. I really am an idiot, aren't I? A silly old costume-maker with her favourites. But I just wanted to make sure that you really understood. I don't know if I managed to get my point across.'

'I think so,' said Zoe.

'There was another thing I wanted to say. It's important to love – to love people and to love what you do. But it's also important to *be* loved. That's something we all need, so that we can make our way in the world, so that we can be strong. Sometimes, when you don't feel that you're loved enough, it's hard to cope with everyday things. Now, now, don't pull that face. I just wanted to mention it, and I'm sure that it's not the case with you. You've got a lovely family and loads of friends, haven't you? And this silly old grouch loves you too.'

Zoe smiled at her and took a step forward, as if to hug her, only she couldn't, because the ironing board and its rustling load were in the way. But it felt like a hug anyway.

Afterwards, when she was on her own again, Zoe thought back to her conversation with Demetra. It was strange because they'd talked about such important things, and even now she wasn't sure that she'd really understood. Above all, she wasn't sure why she'd gone to ask Demetra that particular question. After all, even if Leda had fallen for Leo and couples were popping up all over the place, what did it really matter to her?

Oh, of course it mattered to her. But why? Did she want to be like everyone else because it was easier that way? Zoe didn't like to think of herself as a sheep. Or was it because she wanted Roberto to wait for her and hold her hand and walk with her whenever they had to go from one room to another? How confusing it all was. She really wanted things to be simple, just like they were a year ago, or even a few months ago, before the summer, when the most important thing had been the end-of-year recital, and then the exam. Those things had depended on her, on what she was like, on how she behaved. These affairs of the heart seemed so difficult to grasp, and so complicated. But maybe, Zoe thought, it was just that she wasn't ready yet.

* * *

That evening, her mum and dad went out to dinner by themselves. They didn't get dressed up, but her mum was wearing a bit more make-up than usual and she looked lovely with her starry eyes and her bright pink lips. Her perfume, orange and vanilla, trailed behind her, and that was unusual too, because you normally had to hug her to smell it, breathing it in from her hair and her throat. They were ready, standing at the door, already wearing their coats.

'Are you celebrating something?' Sara asked them, mischievously.

'No, not really,' their dad answered. 'You don't have to be celebrating something to go out. I'm just celebrating the fact that your mum's so beautiful and that she still manages to put up with me.' He looked at her with a smile.

She smiled back at him and pushed her hair over one ear. 'If that's why we're going out, then I have to say that you're pretty good at putting up with me too,' she replied.

Zoe understood that at that moment, even though their three daughters were standing there, there were actually just the two of them, and they were saying things that only they understood.

Then her mum suddenly became Mum again and said, 'Sara, Zoe, make sure you go to bed at the usual time and don't do anything silly. If there are any problems, give us a call. I'll lock the door, but the keys are there on the table.'

Maria dashed forward to claim the first goodbye hug from mum, then Zoe and Sara each got one too. Dad dished out kisses on their cheeks and they left. Maria zoomed into the living room, turned on the television and started flicking through the channels, looking for cartoons.

'They really like each other, don't they?' Zoe said to Sara. They were still standing out in the hallway.

'Oh no. They love each other,' Sara answered.

'We're lucky, aren't we?'

'Yes. We certainly are,' Sara said.

They looked into each other's eyes. They were both thinking about their friends whose parents were separated or divorced and who were clearly having a hard time of it, even if they were pretending that they weren't.

Then Maria yelled, 'Who's making the popcorn?' and all sad thoughts disappeared.

All that remained was the pleasure of a few hours on their own, eating rubbish and watching a bit more TV than usual.

CHAPTER FIVE

Absences

Maestro Fantin's tuft of white hair wasn't sticking up above the piano the next day at school. And when Madame Olenska indicated that the barre music should start, with a quick tap of her cane, you could also hear that the hands on the keys were not his. The touch was not as gentle, it was more mechanical, as if whoever was playing wasn't actually thinking about the music, but about the exercises, which were always exactly the same repetitive movements. That was a mistake, because it really did make the exercises feel mechanical and dull, and, of course, Madame Olenska noticed immediately.

'Zoe, you're so stiff! Stop working on auto-pilot. *Think.*'

At the end of the lesson, a blonde girl popped up from behind the piano. She nodded at Madame and left the room. Zoe was the last one to leave. She wanted to know what was going on.

'Is Maestro Fantin ill, Madame?'

Madame Olenska looked Zoe up and down, as she always did, as though she was trying to put you in your place. The look she gave always seemed to be saying, 'Stand up straight!'

But her expression was kind when she answered. 'That's right. He's got flu.'

'Have you heard from him? Do you know when he's coming back?'

'Yes, I've heard from him. Not even he knows when he'll be back. At his age, these things can take a long time to get over.'

'Do you think I could give him a call?'

Madame Olenska smiled to herself.

'I should think so. He'll like that. Go to the office and ask them to give you his number. Tell them I said you could have it.'

Maestro Fantin wasn't really a friend as such. It's not easy to be friends with someone who's so much older than you. Zoe saw her proper friends all the time, outside of school as well, but she only ever saw Maestro Fantin in dance class, and sometimes in the corridors. But she'd become fond of him, as she had of Demetra and of certain places in the Academy. They were all things and people that she loved and that were part of her daily life. So that afternoon, when she was back at home, she dialled the number.

'Hello?' A woman's voice answered. It was sweet, but sounded a little hoarse. It was the voice of an old lady.

'Good afternoon,' Zoe replied brightly. 'My name's Zoe. I'm a student at the Ballet Academy. I'd like to speak to Maestro Fantin, if it's not too much trouble.'

'No, dear, it's no trouble at all, if you'll just wait a moment.'

There was the sound of footsteps walking away from the phone, then distant voices, then more footsteps approaching.

Then there was the voice of someone with a sore throat saying, 'Hello, Zoe. How nice to hear from you.'

'Are you feeling better, Maestro Fantin?' Zoe asked.

'Oh, I don't know. Nothing's hit me this hard for years. I feel like a little child again.' And he laughed, with a deep, rasping sound. 'My wife keeps squeezing fruit juice for me, and giving me lots to drink, and she sits by my bedside and tells me stories about when we were young. And after a while, I fall asleep. How are you doing? Is everything okay at school?'

'Yes, everything's pretty quiet. Your replacement's really bad at playing the piano, though. It's not like she actually makes mistakes, it's just that it's ... something else.'

'She's young, and maybe she's bored. I imagine she'd

rather be giving a concert.'

'But she's no good,' Zoe repeated.

'When you're young, you imagine that you can do all kinds of things,' Maestro Fantin told her gently. 'I wanted to be a concert pianist myself. I actually was, for a while. Then I got married and I didn't like being so far away from home all the time. So I gave it up. I started giving lessons to children and then along came the Academy. And so time passes.' A coughing fit forced him to stop talking.

Between coughs, he managed to say, 'Well, thanks for calling, Zoe,' and she understood that it was time to hang up and say goodbye, so she did just that.

How strange. She'd never thought of Maestro Fantin as someone who could have had a different life than the one he had now, as someone who might have had dreams and then given them up. He still seemed to be happy, though. People who gave up on their dreams shouldn't be happy, should they? But maybe the sadness went away as they got older . . .

The next day, Maestro Fantin's absence was felt even more strongly. Charlotte, the substitute, had to play an easy waltz, the one they always used for their pirouettes, but she played it too quickly and no one could keep up.

Madame Olenska banged her cane on the floor and the music stopped. In a loud voice she said, 'Charlotte, that's enough for today. You may go.'

Charlotte stood up, looking flushed and embarrassed, and fled. Things went better with the CD. Its reliable performance met with Madame's approval and the lesson continued without any hitches.

Zoe liked doing pirouettes and the strange sensation they gave her – when she watched other people do them or pictured herself doing them. She imagined a complete loss of control, like when she was little and spun round and round and got dizzy and fell over. But when ballerinas did pirouettes, falling over was not an option. Zoe had learned to choose a point and to keep looking at it and coming back to look at it after every whirl around, and as long as she stuck to that, she was practically guaranteed not to fall over. Whether she always performed elegant pirouettes, though, that was another matter entirely.

As always, whenever it was a question of pure technique, Laila was the best. She was like Coppélia, the inventor's mechanical daughter. Zoe had seen the ballet on DVD and for real at the theatre last year too, and she could clearly remember the perfect robotic actions that the ballerina had expressed so well. But in *Coppélia* it was on purpose. Laila lacked expression. It didn't seem as though the school required them to show any expression. It wasn't a subject that they were tested on and given a grade for. And anyway, thought Zoe, I'm not the teacher, so it's not my place to judge.

Most of the boys were pretty good at doing pirouettes. It was all about strength, athletic ability and skill. For the boys, grace and strength had to go hand in hand, to blend together and become as one. Lucas was really great, as usual. Leo only just managed – he seemed a bit nervous. Madame Olenska was bound to give him an hour of extra exercises. But Roberto was absolutely wonderful. His muscles were perfectly defined in his long, slim legs. His body was beautifully proportioned. Every limb made a clean line, each gesture was precise. As he whirled around like a spinning top – he seemed like a perfect mixture of grace and strength, like the elegant cologne Zoe's father sometimes wore.

I can't be the only one who sees him that way, can I? Zoe wondered as she left the class, still a little out of breath after the exercise. *It's not just that I see him the way I want him to be, is it? Might that be true of other things as well? Is he really nice or do I just think he is? Is he really funny or do I just concentrate so hard on thinking that he's funny that he actually becomes funny? Maybe I'm the only one who's laughing.*

She had many questions. It was so confusing, this love stuff and trying to think about love made her head spin. It was such a huge, serious word. Was this love, or a crush? If love was a colour, what colour would it be? Would it be red or pink, like hearts and sweets and that kind of thing? No. Zoe suddenly decided that the word 'love' was blue, like one of those big, bright springtime skies, the sort that they hadn't seen for some time now and which wouldn't be coming back for a while. And of course it was just a coincidence that Roberto's eyes were blue.

The weeks passed by quickly and the weather was colder now. Zoe and Leda still weren't really as close as they used to be. Sitting together on the bus, bumping against each other as the bus jerked and lurched, they were barely talking, and felt awkward around each other.

One day Leda sighed. She turned to Zoe and, very quietly, said, 'I'm sorry.'

Zoe heard her perfectly well, but it was actually quite noisy on the bus, what with the passengers chattering and the sound of the traffic, so she said, 'What did you say?'

Leda took a deep breath, swallowed and repeated herself. 'I'm sorry. I've been a bit of an idiot lately. I went to Paula's house the other day, because she invited me over for dinner, and she was going on and on and on about boys this, boys that and boys the other, and well, I just got bored in the end. She's so stupid. I mean, I'm interested in boys, but that really is all she ever talks about.'

'So what would you prefer to talk about then?' Zoe asked her.

Leda didn't pick up on the sarcastic tone in Zoe's voice.

'Oh, I don't know . . . clothes, film, books . . .' Then she looked into Zoe's eyes and added, with a little giggle, 'And boys.'

'Exactly!' Zoe grinned. 'Go on then, let's talk about boys.'

'Okay, but first let me tell you something. You know what I don't like about Paula? It's that she never listens. She always has to be the one who's talking, but you're really good at listening.'

'So I just need to keep my ears open and listen to you then?'

'Oh, come on, Zoe. You know what I mean. You listen for a bit and then I listen for a bit. We take it in turns.'

Then Leda started talking about Leo. Apparently he kept looking at her in a certain way and yesterday he'd asked her to lend him her history notes so he could check that he'd got everything down properly, and it had to mean something that she was the one he asked, didn't it?

'Maybe he asked you because you're one of the best in the class at history,' suggested Zoe, and even as she was saying it she realised that being honest can sometimes seem a lot like being spiteful.

'Well, then he could have asked you, couldn't he?' snapped Leda, and Zoe also realised that sometimes spitefulness just popped out, without you thinking about it.

But she didn't have much time to think about that because Leda carried on talking, and she talked and talked and talked until they reached Zoe's stop. She told Zoe about Leo's beautiful hands, his eyelashes, and how beautiful his voice was.

Zoe looked out of the window into the darkness that was studded with a thousand lights, from cars and street-lamps and illuminated signs, and thought that maybe, sooner or later, she would become that boring and fixated too, and then she'd be pleased to have a close friend who could listen to her and put up with her as she was having to do with Leda.

The next day, everyone realised that it had been two whole weeks since Alissa had been at school.

'She's got tonsillitis,' said Sophie, who sat next to her in class. 'It's too painful to eat, so she's lost quite a bit of weight, just like that.'

At the end of the lesson, the English teacher made an announcement.

'I need someone to take Alissa some work. Phoning her won't be enough, because there are some exercises to give to her. If she doesn't do them, she's going to fall too far behind. Any volunteers?'

Leda immediately put her hand up and dragged Zoe's hand into the air as well. 'We'll go. We live in the same part of town as her.'

Afterwards, in the corridor, Zoe said to Leda, 'You could at least have asked me if I wanted to go.'

'We're doing her a favour, aren't we?' Leda said.

But Zoe suspected that Leda had another motive, and she was right.

Alissa's mum opened the door and smiled at the girls.

'Come in, come in. How kind of you. Alissa's waiting for you in the living room.' In the bright light of the entrance hall, she looked tired and drawn, as if she was ill as well.

Alissa was sitting on a small red sofa beside the window. She was wearing a green-and-white tracksuit, which, like most tracksuits in the world, should have made her look like the Michelin man, and yet it didn't, it just hung off her body. She looked like a badly dressed scarecrow. Her face was really hollow and thin as well.

'Is your sore throat better now?' said Leda, but even that was too much.

'Shh,' answered Alissa, very quietly, but her voice wasn't the voice of someone with a sore throat – it was a voice of deep exhaustion.

'When are you coming back to school?' Zoe asked, handing her the schoolwork.

'I don't know,' said Alissa, looking out of the window.

'Well, you're not missing much. They just keep giving us tests in class and Madame Olenska is in a really bad mood at the moment. We can't do anything right. It's awful!' Leda said, pulling a face. 'The other day she even yelled at Laila, and you know that only ever happens once in a blue moon. Hey, I wonder if there's a blue moon out there now.'

Leda looked out of the window. There wasn't a blue moon, but there was a gentle flickering against the yellow light of a streetlamp.

'Hey, look, it's snowing!'

In an instant, all three of them were kneeling on the sofa, with their noses glued to the window. They stayed there, just staring, for a while. Then Zoe turned to look at Alissa's sharp profile and her hand resting on the back of the red sofa – her fingers were so long and thin. Zoe had seen an advert in the newspaper for some rings studded with tiny diamonds. The model had such perfect model's hands that she'd managed to fit seven rings on to her ring finger. Zoe had looked at her own hands and calculated that she couldn't fit more than three on to hers. You could probably get about eight on Alissa's finger.

'Okay then, I guess we'll be off,' said Leda after a while.

Alissa smiled a tired smile that made her cheekbones stick out even more. She didn't get up to say goodbye. She just turned around and slumped down on the sofa, like a deflated balloon.

Outside, the snow was still floating down. It was so thin that it didn't lie on the ground or even on the car windows, but that didn't matter. Zoe looked up into the sky until her eyes were filled with little swirling dots as they fell slowly on their unpredictable paths.

'Anorexia,' said Leda as they were waiting for the bus. 'She's the first one in our class.'

'Do you think so?' asked Zoe. 'Why hasn't anyone else said so?'

'She's always been really skinny. She's the thinnest of all of us. She only ever has yogurt and fruit for lunch, and she won't even eat every kind of fruit. No bananas. Or pears. Too much sugar. Apples are okay, and kiwis, and oranges, and mandarins and . . .'

The list was too long and stupid and Zoe stopped listening to Leda. She was thinking that the nutritionist would soon be paying another visit to the school. She came once a year to give them a lecture about the importance of a healthy, balanced diet as a foundation for a career as a dancer. However, a couple of girls had to leave the school every year because of eating disorders, so it seemed that not everyone really listened to what she said. Leda was right. It had never happened in their class before – but they were still children. Well, they had been children until the other day, when Kai had called them 'ladies and gentlemen'. So, they were growing up, and growing up brought certain dangers with it.

'I like bananas too much, anyway. I don't think I could give them up,' continued Leda, lost in her world of healthy fruit and sugary fruit. 'Only if they're still a bit green, though. The squishy brown ones with spots are disgusting. Her parents will make sure she gets the help she needs, and she'll start eating better again, you'll see. Anyway, got to go!'

Zoe waved goodbye. It was such an effort being patient with Leda at the moment. If it weren't for the fact that Zoe was so fond of her . . . It dawned on Zoe that it was possible to like a person in spite of that person's behaviour, rather than because of it. And it wasn't as if she wanted to just change her friends overnight, was it?

She wondered how Alissa had let herself become so ill. Maybe she didn't have a close friend to tell her that she shouldn't try to make herself thin by giving up food. Maybe she didn't have a real friend who could support her and like her, but who could also give her a good talking-to when she needed it, like with Zoe and Leda. For a moment, Zoe felt lucky. As she got off at her stop and stepped into the tiny flakes of snow, she felt sorry that she'd become so irritated by Leda.

CHAPTER SIX

A Visit

'Can I come and watch while you're having your dance lesson?'

Zoe was talking to Alice on the phone. Alice was coming to visit an aunt and she was staying nearby for the weekend and Monday, because Monday was a teacher-training day at her school. She was really excited and couldn't wait to tell Zoe, so now they were making plans and coming up with ideas. Zoe knew that the rules at the Academy were really strict and that no one was allowed to come and watch the lessons, not even mums and dads.

'I'm sorry,' she said, 'but I don't think that'll be possible.'

'Oh. I was really looking forward to it.'

She could hear the disappointment in Alice's voice.

'There might be something else we could do. I'm not promising anything, though,' said Zoe. 'We'll have to wait and see.'

Instead of dashing down the corridor along with everyone else the next morning during break, Zoe went up the stairs to the offices.

She knocked on the door of the secretary's office and waited for the intimidating 'Enter!'

Elsa, the school secretary, was a legend, a myth of meanness beyond compare. She sat entrenched behind an imposing desk, with two palm plants framing her like a fake oasis. She had very high, very black hair, woven into a structure that looked like a small tower; tiny, flinty black eyes, behind deep-blue spectacle frames that looked like a diamante-sprinkled butterfly. A scarf, also blue, was draped around her neck. She looked like a big, strange, brightly coloured insect staring at you, ready to pounce, Zoe thought.

Zoe cleared her throat and, aware that politeness was everything, said, 'Good morning.'

'Good morning,' replied Elsa curtly, and waited with a very serious look on her face that was not the slightest bit encouraging.

'I wanted to ask you . . .'

'You *wanted* to ask me or do you *still* want to ask me? Did you want to ask me yesterday or do you want to ask me now? Why is it that you children today are incapable of expressing yourselves properly?'

'I want to,' said Zoe.

But that didn't sound very polite, so she corrected herself.

'I would like to. I would like to know if there are two tickets for the Gala rehearsal. I know that it's on Saturday afternoon and I'd like to watch it with a friend of mine.'

'Ah, so that's it,' said Elsa.

She opened up a drawer and took out a folder which she opened in such a way that Zoe couldn't see what was inside, even though she could guess. It was the seating plan for the theatre, with all of the seats and boxes divided into sections of different colours. The people who were usually invited to the rehearsals were journalists, or people with season tickets to the ballet, the true fans. There were also some tickets set aside for pensioners and for clubs. There were never many tickets left over, because they were free, so the few tickets that were available were very much in demand. This was the first time that Zoe had asked for rehearsal tickets. Usually, if there was a show that she really wanted to see, her mum and dad took her to a normal performance, without trying to take any short cuts, but this was a special occasion and it was also true that Zoe couldn't afford to pay for two tickets at the full price herself. So she crossed her fingers and waited.

'Hmm . . . let's see . . .'

Elsa really liked to create a feeling of suspense. She was always like that. Everyone was really frightened of her, but she didn't scare Zoe – she was curious, in fact. This insect was so unpredictable. Would she attack? Or would she keep her distance and just sit there, stroking her feelers?

'Yes,' she said, finally, having allowed the tension to mount for long enough. 'I think that it might be possible to come up with two tickets on this occasion.'

She scribbled some numbers on a card with the crest of the Academy printed on it in red and gold. Then she handed it to Zoe, examining her over the top of her glasses.

'So, are you being a good little girl?' she asked, abruptly.

'That's none of your business. You're not my mum and you're not even one of my teachers,' Zoe said. No, that wasn't true. That's what she wanted to say, but she managed to bite her tongue. She had what she came for, after all. Alice would get to see a real ballet at the Academy Theatre for the first time in her life.

'Yes, Elsa. Thank you,' said Zoe, turning to leave.

'Don't mention it,' the insect's dry voice responded.

Zoe closed the door and went back to join her friends for what was left of break.

Leda immediately took hold of her arm and said, 'Do you want to come to the cinema with us on Saturday? It's the boys, and Paula and Sophie. Do you fancy it? Of course you do.'

'I'm actually doing something on Saturday,' said Zoe. She had her hands in her pockets and she touched the magic card that Elsa had given her.

'Oh . . . That's a shame. I'll have to ask Estelle instead.' Leda detached herself from Zoe's arm and skidded over to join the group that was standing over by the window.

Zoe was left all alone, looking out at the playground with its naked trees and the symphony of greys; grey soil, grey walls, grey sky – a sunless winter day.

Sensing that someone was standing beside her again, she murmured, 'So, is Estelle going with you then?'

'I really would prefer it if you came.'

The voice. *That* voice. Zoe turned around, but slowly, because she knew what she was going to see: Roberto! His face was very close – so close that she could see the almost-white tips of his eyelashes.

'Well, actually, a friend I met on holiday is coming to visit and I've promised to spend some time with her,' said Zoe, then she corrected herself. 'I mean, I want to spend time with her. And I've managed to get hold of two tickets for the rehearsal on Saturday. Alice has never seen a ballet before.'

'I understand,' said Roberto. 'But don't think that

you're missing out. I reckon there'll be too many of us to have any real fun. It's not as if the cinema's going anywhere, is it? Maybe . . .'

Zoe waited, her heart thumping away a little faster in her chest, as though there were a little man in there who had had a sudden burst of energy and doubled the speed of his work. Maybe what?

'Maybe we could go somewhere next week on our own, just you and me. If your mum and dad will let you, I mean.'

Oh yes, her mum and dad. Zoe hadn't thought about that aspect. Of course, if they were going out in a group of six, seven, eight, her parents wouldn't object. But if it was just her and Roberto? She shrugged her shoulders, as though to shake off that annoying thought and concentrate on the good part. Roberto had asked her out! To go somewhere on their own! Just the two of them! She smiled at him, without any hesitation.

'That would be lovely. I'll ask them.'

And then the bell went and Jamie came running up and gave Roberto a whack on the back. Roberto whipped around and thumped him in the belly, but not too hard, just messing around. They were like a couple of bear cubs, thought Zoe. They had the same gentle clumsiness. Almost furtively, she walked away and headed for the classroom, with one treasure in her pocket and another one warming her heart.

Alice dressed for winter was not the same as Alice dressed for summer, even though, when you were in the mountains, you sometimes had to wrap yourself up, even in August. There, it sometimes felt as though the season was changing from one hour to the next. In the same day, you'd go from having bare arms to wearing lots of layers, to wearing bare arms again.

Bare arms certainly weren't an option now, though. Alice was wearing a long red quilted winter coat, which was wrapped around her like a cocoon, with a matching scarf, gloves and hat which was red with a pattern of reindeer and snowflakes on. Underneath she was wearing jeans that flared a bit too much at the bottom, a top that was a bit too tight and showed some of her tummy (brrr, how chilly!) and a pair of shoes with wedges that were a bit too rubbery-looking. But that was just Zoe's opinion, so it didn't really count, and, anyway, everyone knows that people in different parts of the country do things differently.

'Will I look okay for the theatre like this? I haven't brought much to wear with me. You know what it's like when you travel by train. But I've got a black top with sparkles on, to dress up. Your room's beautiful. So's your house. Wow, you and your sisters are so lucky to have your own rooms. My brothers share a bedroom. And my room's about half the size of this. Hey, what a lovely view!

What time do we have to leave to get there on time? Who's taking us? Or are we going on our own?'

Even though Alice said such a lot, it wasn't an annoying torrent of the kind that Leda had been coming out with recently. Alice spoke like that because her emotions were running away with her. She was obviously completely wrapped up in what she was feeling and wanted to tell Zoe and to share it with her. Zoe tried to follow her jumble of thoughts and questions and to respond as well as she could.

'Don't worry, a rehearsal isn't the same thing as an opening night. You can wear what you like. And thank you. That's very nice of you. Yes, it's true, the house is big. We'll leave here at two. The rehearsal starts at three. We're going on our own. It's not a difficult journey.'

Zoe felt happy. She looked at the smiling face of her holiday friend. She looked different without a tan, but that just made her deep-blue eyes look even more blue, and she noticed that her hair was paler and curlier around the hairline, almost like little feathers.

'I missed you, you know,' Zoe said and her words came directly from her heart, so directly that she didn't even have time to think them.

'I missed you too. I really did. You could have written a bit more often, though. Or didn't you have enough time?'

'I'm sorry, you're absolutely right. I just never seemed to find the time. I don't think I'm very good at writing letters and texts are hopeless.'

'You've got a computer, haven't you? Of course you have. I'm getting one for Christmas, so we can send each other emails. They don't take so long to write. You're right about text messages, you can't really use them to communicate. Will you show me your clothes? What do you usually do at the weekend?'

Standing in front of the open wardrobe, with Alice nosing through her jumpers and rifling through her T-shirts, Zoe thought about how she didn't usually do much at the weekend – although actually that weekend she'd had a choice of things to do. Of course, she couldn't say that to Alice, because it might make her feel guilty, and then, of course, she'd want to know all about Roberto. Zoe didn't really have much to say about him and she preferred to keep what little she did have to herself. Leda said that Anna had told her everything, about noses and tongues and about how to kiss, and she said that she understood everything a lot better now.

Zoe thought that if Roberto kissed her, she wouldn't tell anyone. Actually, that wasn't true – she might tell Alice, but perhaps only because Alice lived so far away and she didn't know Roberto and she couldn't keep on asking her all about what it was like. Even if she asked her in an email, Zoe could always give a vague answer, couldn't she? If Roberto ever did kiss her, that was.

'Hello? Earth to Zoe!' Alice was waving a hand in front of Zoe's eyes and grinning.

Zoe smiled back at her. 'Sorry. I was miles away.'

'You know your clothes are awful! I didn't find a single thing in there that was even vaguely fashionable. Don't you ever read magazines? Or look at adverts? Do you even notice what other girls are wearing? What time did you say the rehearsal finishes?'

'At six.'

'And the Academy is in the centre of town, isn't it? Of course it is, I can answer that question for myself. So, after the show, we'll go for a little wander around the shops. You bring some money and I'll give you some fashion advice. I think just two new pieces should do the trick.'

It sounded as though it was going to be a very busy afternoon. Zoe fell back on to the bed with a little bounce.

'Alice, do you know how to calm down and do nothing for just five minutes?' she said, smiling.

The Gala of the Stars was absolutely wonderful. It was the final rehearsal, which was almost like the opening night, except the occasional mistake was allowed. Alice went into raptures about all of the gold and the beautiful decorations and the red velvet in the theatre.

She stared in amazement at the ushers in their elegant black uniforms with gold braid. 'They look like really posh waiters, don't they?' she remarked.

Before the show started she wanted to go and look into the orchestra pit to watch the musicians taking up position and tuning their instruments. 'It's crazy, isn't it? Look at them, they just come in on the bus, like it's nothing special, and then they come in here and play such amazing music. You can't really call that work, can you? What a fantastic job!'

Once they'd sat down, she took a really good look all around the theatre, and examined every one of the boxes as though she expected them to be full of kings and queens. 'Do you recognise that woman over there? No? Are you sure? I think she might be famous.'

Alice just stared and stared at the huge chandelier with its crystal drops. When the show started, she finally closed her mouth, but she carried on sighing and whenever anything really special happened she held her breath, so she still managed to comment on everything that absolutely needed to be commented upon, even without saying a word.

First to dance were a couple of Russian ballerinas. It was fairly traditional, but they were dressed as black swans, with a lot of gold trim, and that was enough to make Alice swoon with pleasure. Then came Mariah Simone's moment with *Noblesse*, and once again Zoe reminded herself that it really was worth the effort of all that studying if there was even a remote possibility of becoming like her. That was true *Noblesse* – nobility – up there on the stage, dressed in shades of violet, stretched into extreme positions, making the body talk with its special language of muscles and motion. *Noblesse*, Zoe thought, meant doing well at the things that you loved – so well that you approached perfection and brought joy to the people who watched you. Zoe almost clapped her hands raw when Mariah Simone had finished. She sneaked a look at Alice and saw that the piece had created a similar effect on her, because her cheeks were flushed, as though she'd been running.

Julia Monda, wearing Demetra's detested pink tutu, also put on a good show, but her piece was a sequence of very traditional steps. Okay, she did them absolutely impeccably, but really it was nothing special, Zoe thought.

During the interval, Alice asked Zoe who she had thought was better, and of course Zoe said Mariah Simone, and Alice said, 'Yes, but I found it easier to understand the dance that the one in pink did. She's more of a real ballerina, isn't she?'

This could have been a very interesting discussion but they'd gone to the bar for an orange juice and it was pretty chaotic. They had to move away from the counter to avoid all of the elbowing, so the conversation remained unfinished.

The second, more modern, part of the show was good fun. There was an Argentinean dancer who was all leaps and athletic strength, and an African dancer with a beautiful body, which seemed to be carved from ebony, so there was a lot to look at, even though the dances were very simple and the costumes, as Demetra had complained, were almost non-existent.

After the gala, Zoe remembered that they were supposed to be going somewhere else. She had hoped that Alice would be too tired, but no. Alice steered her right out of the theatre and, once they were outside, she said, 'Which way to the shops?'

Five minutes later, they were amongst the insane crush of Saturday evening shoppers, weaving their way through gangs of teenagers, ladies in thick coats and couples with buggies.

'Here, I think this is the right place,' announced Alice, stopping in front of the huge glass doors of a big department store that had recently opened. She headed inside dragging Zoe behind her, said hello to the security guard as if she knew him, and then strode up the grand marble staircase.

'But the children's department is downstairs,' Zoe protested.

'So you think we're children, do you?' said Alice, shaking her head as though Zoe was a hopeless case.

Zoe had thought that it would be hard to find the right sizes in the women's department, but, just looking around, she could tell that it wasn't going to be a problem. There were loads of tiny little T-shirts and tops hung alongside skirts and trousers that were just about big enough to fit a stick insect. Alice dived into the rows of clothes racks and resurfaced triumphantly waving a velvet jacket in a pretty shade of pink with laces up the back, like an old-fashioned corset.

'Look. How about this? And it only costs thirty-nine pounds.'

Zoe had thirty-nine pounds. In fact, she had eighty pounds that she'd been saving up, so she also bought herself a black sleeveless top with a high neckline, which she thought was quite acceptable, even if it was a little short on the tummy, perhaps; in many ways it was quite similar to the leotards they wore at school, except for the neckline. To complete the outfit, she bought a denim mini-skirt that was very dark, almost black.

'You've got some ballerina shoes, haven't you? Ha ha, well, if you haven't, who has?' Alice laughed. 'You'll need black ones, I think. If you wear them with opaque black tights, you'll look absolutely fabulous.'

'Aren't you going to buy anything?' Zoe asked her.

'I didn't bring any money,' Alice said, shrugging her shoulders. So Zoe spent her remaining nine pounds and ninety-nine pence on an orange top that Alice couldn't take her eyes off.

After that, they had to face the crowds again. They linked arms and moved forwards through the pushing, surging waves of people, like a little commando unit, standing shoulder to shoulder against the world. They didn't talk because they wouldn't have been able to hear anything. Zoe felt good – and almost didn't regret having missed out on the afternoon with Roberto and the others. Besides, she knew that he was right: the group was too big. Two was just the right number for a Saturday afternoon, so, it should be just the two of them or not at all.

Now that Alice was asleep (and snoring slightly) on the airbed beside Zoe's bed, Zoe was going back over the afternoon and, as usual, felt overwhelmed by confusing thoughts. The things that she'd bought were really nice. She'd tried them on all together in front of the mirror at home under the expert eye of Alice, who gave the outfit the final verdict.

'The jacket looks better without the laces tied up; it's okay for the hem of the top to ride up a little; you should keep the skirt low on your hips – don't keep trying to tug it up to your armpits!'

Zoe liked how she'd looked. It had all turned out well, including the look with the black tights and ballerina shoes that Alice had suggested – even though they were summer shoes and she couldn't go out in them now or her feet would freeze.

If there was one thing that most ballerinas had in common, it was a beautiful pair of legs, and, strangely, the black tights hadn't made them look too thin. They actually made her legs seem more feminine and shapely. Mum and Sara, who had come in to have a look when they heard

Alice's squeals of excitement, had both approved as well. Mum had looked a little puzzled, but she'd still smiled. So that part of the day had turned out well, really well.

But something else was troubling Zoe, a doubt that Alice had put into her mind with her comments about ballerinas. What was a real ballerina? Alice had thought that Julia Monda was more of a real ballerina than Mariah Simone. Did that mean that Laila was a real ballerina? Were the Lailas of the world destined for applause and unconditional admiration? Could you ever know? Was it more important what other people thought or how you felt inside?

Because if Zoe believed what Demetra said, Julia Monda didn't feel anything beautiful inside and she was just jealous and rude and mean. But then that did make sense – she danced like a mechanical doll on stage, the look helped by make-up and costumes that transformed her into every little girl's dream. Yes, it made perfect sense. It was her job. And she was very good at it. But Zoe could tell that Mariah Simone was different. For her, dancing wasn't a job and wasn't something that you did and that you were very good at. It was, quite simply, her life. And that was why she was such an extraordinary dancer.

Zoe decided that if she was going to be a ballerina, she wanted to be a Mariah Simone. Not because of the success, but because she wanted to be happy about what she was doing, and she wanted everyone to know just how happy she was.

On Monday morning, Zoe went back to school, after saying goodbye to a sleepy Alice, who was waiting for her parents to come and pick her up and take her home.

The Sunday had been fun as well. They'd gone to the cinema and then to McDonald's, where they'd stuffed themselves with fries. It was just the two of them again, enjoying their independence. But now Zoe really was on her own. She didn't always meet up with Leda on the bus to school, because it was difficult to time it right, but maybe that was just as well.

It had been a lovely weekend, far away from the usual things, from the usual people. She knew it would be difficult to stay close to Alice, because they lived so far apart, but if they could send each other emails after Christmas, maybe that would be a way for them to develop their friendship. At least they could give it a try.

CHAPTER SEVEN

Seeing the Towers

'So, would next Saturday be a good day?'

It was sunny and unusually warm for November, so everybody else had dashed downstairs and into the playground at break that day. However, Roberto had come over to Zoe, and the two of them had hung back, alone together in the corridor.

'That sounds good. I'm free on Saturday. Did you have fun last weekend?'

Roberto pulled a face. 'To start with, we had to queue for half an hour to buy the tickets. Then I didn't even like the film. Afterwards we went to the shopping mall, but it was really crowded and I was so bored that I said goodbye and went home.' It almost sounded like an apology. 'What about you? Did your holiday friend enjoy herself?'

'Yes. It was the first time I'd seen her since August, and it was a bit weird to start with. You know, people are really different in the summer. But we had fun. It was a laugh.'

'I don't know if you've got any thoughts about what you'd like to do on Saturday. I was thinking we could go and see that exhibition: Celestial Towers. My brother went and he said it's beautiful. The only problem is that it's on the outskirts of town. You have to go on two buses and it takes absolutely ages to get there. But if we're not in any hurry . . .'

'Well, we do have all afternoon, don't we?' said Zoe. 'I'd love to go.'

Zoe was quite used to going to exhibitions with her mum and dad. Sometimes they even went on day trips to other cities to visit an exhibition, if it was a particularly good one. But she'd never gone on her own before and she'd never chosen an artist or an exhibition title herself. Of course, she wouldn't be going on her own this time either.

They went down the stairs together, very slowly, without saying anything else. When they reached the playground, a group of girls turned round to look at them and Estelle whispered something in Anna's ear.

During dance class, Zoe thought she could feel a pair of eyes looking at her, but she realised it was probably just her imagination. She couldn't look into the mirror to see whose eyes they were and she obviously couldn't turn round to look, but she could feel a strange tingling sensation of being watched. She tried hard to concentrate. They were working on a brief sequence of *grands jetés* that required a great deal of precision in the take-off and landing. It took all of her attention to make those pirouetting leaps with the necessary lightness, without thudding or slipping as she landed on the floor, and then go straight into a *glissade*. Madame Olenska banged her cane sharply on the floor: one and two, one and two, bam bam, bam bam.

'Get those legs up! I want to see you fly! Lift yourselves higher! Don't stick to the ground like a bunch of farmyard ducklings!'

Zoe wondered where she got those images from. Zoe had already performed her part as a duckling, in flight or in the farmyard, and was now watching the others, a little out of breath. Leda soared into the air, flew, landed, and ran over to Zoe. No one was allowed to talk in lessons and perhaps it was just as well, because Zoe suspected that the eyes that had been drilling into her before were Leda's, and that they were full of curious questions.

Or maybe it had been Roberto . . . He had completed the exercise with perfect confidence and was now standing on the other side of the room, directly opposite Zoe, staring at her – seriously, intently, without batting an eyelid. Who knew how many times he'd looked at her during lessons, in the normal classes and in ballet? And why was it that his gaze now felt so different, so much more intense?

In the changing room, Zoe got dressed as quickly as she could, without even pretending to wait for Leda, who had disappeared to the toilets. She didn't want to be interrogated for the entire bus journey. Instead, she wanted to be alone and savour the pleasure of having received an invitation that was just for her.

That evening, Zoe was finishing her homework (some really dull French grammar exercises) when she heard someone cough. She turned around and saw her mum standing in the doorway, with her hand on the doorframe.

'Can I come in?'

'Of course. I was just revising pronouns.'

'Wow,' said Zoe's mum, pulling a funny face. 'Not one of the most fascinating subjects ever, eh?'

'You're not wrong,' smiled Zoe, pushing the book away. 'Did you want to talk about something?'

'I just wanted to say that I like the things you bought for yourself when you went out with Alice. I really liked them,' her mum said, emphasising her words with a decisive nod. 'They suit you and they're really nice. They're fashionable, but without being too silly. But perhaps it might be better if you tell me next time you want to buy clothes for yourself.'

'It was my money,' replied Zoe, weakly.

'I know. That's not the point. You can use my money too, you know, when you *need* something. It's better to ask me and keep your savings to spend on other things. I don't know, a stereo, an iPod, that kind of thing.'

'But if I use your money that means you decide what I'm allowed to wear, and you come to the shops with me, and . . . You know . . .'

'No. You're not a little girl any more, Zoe. Sara often buys things by herself too. You know that. I just want you to have your own taste, not to be influenced by other people's tastes.'

'But I really do like the things I bought with Alice.'

'I know. And I've already told you that I like them too. Let's just say that it worked out well this time. I really don't mind how you dress, as long as you've chosen it yourself. When I was thirteen, I went through a terrible hippy phase. I just wanted to wear long, flowery skirts, sandals and huge jumpers, most of which I'd stolen from your granddad's wardrobe.'

'And what did he say about that?' asked Zoe, curiously.

'Oh, nothing. He was fine about it. It was your gran who didn't really like it. She wanted me to wear pleated skirts, twin sets, that kind of thing.'

'That's kind of strange. Gran never seems very . . . conventional.'

'You're right, she isn't. It's just that she knew that I

was more of a classic type inside, and she thought that I probably really wanted to be classic on the outside too. And she was right. Hang on a second.'

Zoe's mum went on to the landing. There was the sound of a drawer opening, a pause, then closing again, and her mum returned waving a bundle of photographs. She handed them to Zoe.

'Here you go. See if you can guess which one's me.'

It was no easy task. The photos (a few snapshots of the same scene) showed three girls with identical curly hair and flowing skirts that were different colours, but the same style. The jumpers really were huge. They reached halfway down the girls' thighs, wrapping them all up like some kind of dowdy uniform. They had big, genuine smiles on their faces.

'I think you're this one here,' said Zoe, pointing at the girl in the middle. There seemed to be something familiar about her – maybe the way she was tilting her head to one side and resting it on the palm of her hand.

'Wrong. That one's me,' said her mum, touching the face of the girl on the right. She was the thinnest one with the fairest hair. Her skirt was covered in little pink and purple flowers and her enormous V-neck jumper was blue.

'So, how did things work out with Gran?'

'Well, she was very wise and pretty cunning too. She let me wear whatever I wanted for a few months. That fashion lasted until the summer, and then it was over. I gave the skirts away and let Granddad have his jumpers back. I kept the sandals for the summer, to wear to the beach. And that was the end of that.'

'Then did you move on to a different fashion?'

'Well, a bit, yes. That's only natural. If the spring comes and all of the shop windows are full of little blue cardigans and you really like blue, then you want to buy yourself one, don't you? You pick out what you like best from all of things you see. I'd wear jeans and moccasins, instead of the pleated skirts that your gran said I should wear, and I was happy because I felt comfortable in what I was wearing. It was simple, without too many frills.'

'So, do you think the pink jacket's too frillacious then?' asked Zoe, inventing a new word.

'No, I've already told you. It's really nice. Actually, if it fits me, can I borrow it?'

Zoe's mum was tiny, so she didn't have any trouble fitting into the jacket. It really suited her. 'I'll wear it the next time I go out with your dad,' she said to the mirror.

'Hmm, maybe it's about time you took us out for a meal as well, don't you think?' grumbled Zoe.

'You're right. But if we go out together, who's going to wear the jacket?'

'We'll take it in turns,' said Zoe, smiling.

Her mum gave her a hug. Zoe buried her nose in the new velvet, with its sharp, fresh scent, and thought how wonderful it was to have a mum like hers.

Then she freed herself from the hug and said, 'Mum? Can I ask you something?'

'What is it?' Her mum looked into her eyes.

Goodness, they were the same height now. Zoe had grown much taller, and she hadn't even noticed.

'Can I go out with a friend on Saturday? A boy?'

'A boy? Do I know him?'

'Yes. It's Roberto.'

'Well, if you're allowed to go out on your own with a friend who's a girl, I don't see why you shouldn't be able to go out with a friend who's a boy. I mean, of course, it's not the same thing. That's obvious. But, in theory, yes. And Roberto seems like a very nice boy. Where are you planning to go?'

'We're going to see an exhibition.'

'Oooh . . . interesting.' Her mum smiled a little. 'So he's an art lover, is he?'

'I'm not sure,' replied Zoe, in a very serious voice. 'I don't think that's really the point.'

'No, I understand,' said her mum, nodding. 'Okay then, you can tell me all about it afterwards. About the exhibition, I mean.'

Her mum took off the jacket and carefully hung it up in Zoe's wardrobe. 'Have you decided what you're going to wear?'

'That's easy,' answered Zoe. 'I'm going to give my new clothes their first outing.'

'Good idea,' her mum said. 'So it's my turn to stay at home on Saturday afternoon, if the jacket's going out to have fun!'

In the end, Zoe didn't end up wearing the entire new outfit, because it was pouring with rain on Saturday morning – so it wasn't really the right weather for a mini-skirt. Instead she wore a pair of jeans, with black boots. It looked really good.

When Roberto came round to pick her up, she'd been ready and waiting for twenty minutes and was so nervous that she'd managed to chew off all of her lip-gloss. Luckily, it had stopped raining, and though it was damp, it wasn't too cold. He was waiting downstairs in the entrance hall. They smiled at each other and then walked to the bus stop, talking about normal things: homework, films, that kind of thing.

It took them a really long time to get to the exhibition. After the first bus, they had to change and wait for another, and this one crawled across half the city. They weren't in a hurry so they didn't notice how much time it was taking until they got off and realised that it was beginning to get dark. It was quite a long way from the bus stop to the exhi-bition, but it was a nice walk through an old industrial estate, with neatly ordered streets and factories and offices lit with white lights that made the square shapes of the buildings look a little sinister. There was no need to be scared though, because they were surrounded by other people who were also heading to the exhibition – couples of different ages and a group of older girls who were chatting away.

Roberto took Zoe's hand and she noticed that his was cold and dry. She looked up at him (he was a bit taller than her), but she couldn't see much, because they were in the dark space between one lamppost and the next, so she just had to make do with imagining the face she knew.

The exhibition was in an old industrial space that had been stripped of machinery. It was vast and cold and echoed like an aircraft hangar. And there were the towers: seven of them. They were strange constructions made out of rough cement, as if they'd survived a bomb attack or someone had made them from the broken remains of walls. Some of them had neon writing on the sides, like signs on bars or shops, but the words felt magic and important: *Dreams, Stars, Sun, Desires.*

They walked as far as they could around those grey giants inside the black cavern of the building, looking at them from lots of different angles. When they left the exhibition they discovered that it was colder inside the exhibition hall than it was outside. Still holding hands, they walked back to the bus stop and then took the two buses home. Some of the time they talked, some of the time they said nothing. When Roberto disentangled his fingers from hers to wave goodbye as she stood by her front door, Zoe realised that her hand had felt better where it was before.

CHAPTER EIGHT

Celebrations

A week before the end of term, Leda placed a small package tied up with a bow on the bench beside Zoe and hesitantly pushed it towards her. 'Go on,' she whispered. 'Take it. It's for your birthday. I know it's early, but I couldn't wait to give it to you.'

Zoe usually had a party for her birthday, which was just before Christmas. It was important to Zoe that everybody treated her birthday seperately and didn't just give her one present for both, instead of the two she deserved. She hadn't exactly chosen to be born in December. Having a party meant that she got lots of presents, of course, because everyone felt that they had to bring something. Instead of clubbing together to buy one present (even though that did sometimes mean bigger and better presents), Zoe preferred it when everyone turned up with an individual present.

But this year she didn't feel like it. Her mum had asked her if she wanted a party, but she'd had a trace of doubt in her voice. She wondered if Zoe, now that she was more grown up, still wanted to have a little girl party.

Her mum's tone of voice wouldn't have been enough to dissuade Zoe if she'd been really convinced, but she already had some doubts of her own. She'd recently been feeling that she didn't enjoy loud and noisy parties with lots of people any more. She'd rather invite just two or three people to have tea and cakes at a posh café in town.

Zoe thanked her mum, but said that she wasn't planning to have a big party that year, but would rather have a tea party instead. Of course, she knew who she was going to invite to tea. Roberto was first on the list, and then Lucas. And Leda, of course. That was it. She might ask Alice, but of course there was no way she'd be able to come.

Zoe took the parcel Leda had given her and felt the crispness of the paper under her fingertips. 'I'll open it at home on the actual day, if that's all right,' she said to Leda, who was watching her expectantly.

Leda sighed. 'Oh, okay,' she said. 'I hope you like it.'

Zoe found out just how patient she could be, because

Leda's parcel stayed wrapped until the morning of her birthday, which, luckily enough, was on a Saturday. Leda had given her a little pink bear that was hugging a heart-shaped cushion in its paws, with the words *You're my best friend!* embroidered on it. Zoe, still in bed, smiled and put it on her pillow. Then she snuggled back down under the covers to enjoy the lazy morning.

But she didn't really get much of a chance – someone was already knocking at her bedroom door. Without waiting for a response, Maria rushed in, dived on to her bed, bumping Zoe with her knees, and yelled out, 'Happy birthday!'

The others followed her: Mum, Dad and Sara, who was holding a parcel in her hands. 'Happy birthday! Happy birthday!' They sang a rather rowdy version of *Happy Birthday* and Zoe sat up in bed and laughed. She loved her family so much.

'Go on, then. Open it!' Sara said to her, giving the parcel to Zoe.

Inside the parcel was a new *cache-coeur* wrap-around top – one of those special cardigans that cross over at the front and tie up around your waist, which ballerinas wear on top of their leotards before the lesson and sometimes during the breaks so that their muscles don't get cold. It was pink. Beneath it was another *cache-coeur*, in an identical design, but this one was clearly not intended for classes at the Academy, because it was very dark grey with a border of shiny cylindrical beads sewn all around the neckline and other beads scattered here and there on the soft wool.

'Do you like it? Do you like it? I picked it out with Mum,' shouted Maria.

'Actually, we chose it together,' Sara added.

'I liked the contrast between the shiny beads and the dark colour,' their mum said. 'It's pretty, isn't it?'

'It's really going to suit you,' said their dad, smiling.

He was right. Zoe looked at herself in the mirror before she went out that afternoon and really liked what she saw. It was a bit chilly but she decided not to wear a hat. Her freshly washed hair fell softly on to her shoulders like a shiny curtain. Then Leda, Lucas and Roberto arrived, and she greeted them with hugs and kisses, before the four of them set off for the café.

It was full of middle-aged couples and grannies with smartly dressed grandchildren. The café was truly elegant. There was gleaming wood and mirrors and crystal chandeliers. The cake counter extended into the room like a beautiful island of daintily coloured treasures.

'Maybe we should have gone to a fast-food place,' Lucas whispered, as he looked around, feeling somewhat intimidated.

'No, definitely not,' said Zoe. 'I chose this place on purpose, precisely because it's so old. Maybe one hundred years ago today there were four young people just like us who came out to have tea on a Saturday afternoon.'

'I don't think so,' said Roberto. 'A hundred years ago children like us wouldn't have been allowed out alone. Whenever they did go out, they always had an escort with them: Mama, Papa and their governess. What a pain!'

'Oh, look over there!' said Leda, staring at the door.

Laila came in with her mum and dad and they sat down at a corner table, quite a long way from Zoe and her friends – fortunately.

'So what should we do now?' said Leda.

'What do you mean? What do you think we should be doing?' Lucas asked her.

'That's just it,' said Leda. 'I don't know. I've got no idea. Should we pretend there's nothing going on and hope they don't notice us? Or should we go over and say hello?'

'I'll deal with it,' said Zoe. Watched by three pairs of astonished eyes, she pushed back her chair, stood up and went over to the table where Laila was sitting. Zoe talked to Laila and then returned to the others.

The waiter arrived at their table, and they had all the excitement of choosing what they were going to eat. Once they had finished, they all looked meaningfully at Zoe.

'I just asked her if she wanted to come and sit with us,' Zoe sighed. 'You're such a nosy bunch.'

'And she said . . .' Lucas began.

Roberto answered his question. 'No,' he said. 'That's pretty obvious, because she's sitting over there and we're here.'

'She said no *thank you*. She said she didn't want to intrude,' said Zoe. 'But that she was pleased to have been invited.'

'Mademoiselle Perfect gave a model answer, I see. She must have been reading a manual on good manners,' murmured Leda.

'Just imagine what a pain it would have been if she'd said yes and come over and sat with us. I never know what to say to her,' said Lucas.

'But you've never really spoken to her,' Roberto pointed out.

'That's true,' said Lucas, looking rather surprised.

'Well, you're not missing out on much,' said Leda. 'She only ever talks about herself and about how good she is at doing this and that and the other.'

Just then, their orders arrived and so they turned their attention to the steaming cups of tea and the melt-in-your-mouth cakes and the discussion of Laila was closed. Zoe looked over at her table. Laila had her back towards them, so she couldn't see her. Her mum and dad were deep in conversation and they didn't seem to be paying much attention to Laila. Maybe she was bored. Perhaps she was like one of those little girls from a hundred years ago, with an escort even on Saturday afternoon, never free to do what she wanted. Zoe realised just how lucky she was to be able to go out and do even something as simple as have tea with her friends. She also felt a twinge of guilt because she'd been relieved when Laila didn't accept her invitation. Zoe's feelings about Laila made her a bit uncomfortable.

'Mmm.' Lucas opened his eyes wide, with his mouth full. He swallowed and then said, 'Have you tried the cream puffs?'

'I prefer the little sponge cakes,' said Roberto, munching away on his third one.

Zoe had ordered two round cakes covered in pink icing. She gulped them down greedily, one after the other.

Leda chose the cakes that had no cream in 'because they're less fattening,' but as she was already on her seventh, her calorie count was still going to be pretty high! The tea felt like silk as it slipped down Zoe's throat.

'It's all terribly British, isn't it?' Roberto said after a while.

'Well, you're making a good attempt at it for an Italian!' Lucas joked.

'Oh, boys, haven't you forgotten something?' Leda said, giving them a look.

'Oh, yeah, of course,' said Lucas, diving into the pocket of his coat, which was hanging from the back of the chair. After much rummaging, he triumphantly placed a square red box on the bright white tablecloth and pushed it over to Zoe. 'That's from me and Roberto.'

Zoe smiled and opened the box. Inside was a bracelet – a silver chain with a single pearl in the middle, in a delicate shade of pink.

'Happy birthday,' said Lucas and Roberto at the same time.

Leda went 'ooh' and then said, 'It's a river pearl. Can you see that it's not perfectly round, but has little bumps? Hasn't it got a beautiful sheen?' She picked up the bracelet and ran it through her fingers. 'Come on. Give me your wrist and I'll put it on for you,' she said to Zoe.

The silver chain was very delicate and flashed subtly on Zoe's skin.

'It's really beautiful,' said Zoe, looking from Lucas to Roberto.

She wondered who had chosen it, whose idea the present was and, with a very slight feeling of bitterness, whether she might not have preferred two separate presents, so that she could read a secret message into what Roberto had given her.

'Look, they're going,' whispered Leda.

They all looked over at the corner table, where Laila and her parents were putting their coats on.

'Bye,' Leda called across the room, so loud that everyone in the quiet café turned round to look at her. She waved her hand melodramatically, like in one of those film farewells at the railway station.

Laila shyly raised her hand in response to the waves of the others, who had joined in with Leda. Then Laila and her parents left.

They all fancied another cup of tea, and by the time they'd finished drinking it, there wasn't a single crumb left on their plates, even though they'd had so many to start with. Zoe paid with the money that her mum and dad had given her for her birthday tea.

When they left, they found that something was falling from the sky. It wasn't just rain, but a kind of wet blanket that clung to everything. Zoe put up the hood of her coat so that her hair didn't turn into a limp, dripping mess.

'We'll come back with you,' Lucas said. Zoe wondered if she'd imagined the brief frown that Leda seemed to direct at him.

Then Leda said, in a voice as sweet as honey, 'Lucas, don't you remember that you promised to come with me into town and look for that CD? I really have to get it today. Do you mind if we split up? Maybe we can have a chat tomorrow, Zoe. Bye!' She dragged an astonished Lucas away towards the centre of town.

Zoe and Roberto were on their own.

'I'll take you home then,' he said, and it wasn't a question or a suggestion.

Since it was Saturday, it took about a hundred years for

the bus to arrive, but neither of them minded. He took her hand, as he'd done when they went to see the Towers. She squeezed his hand in response. They barely said a word. On the bus, they found two seats together and managed to sit down without having to let go of each other's hands. Zoe leaned her head on his shoulder, almost without intending to – it just seemed to come naturally to her. The bus bumped along through the dark, wet city, but Zoe felt as though they were travelling on a cloud.

Later, in front of Zoe's house, Roberto let go of Zoe's hand.

'Wait a moment,' he said, and he reached into the pocket of his black jeans. 'Here, *this* is my present. The real one.'

It was another box, a blue one this time. Zoe held her breath as she opened it. Inside was a pair of tiny silver earrings – they each had a star with a short chain and then another star in blue enamel.

'I noticed that you had pierced ears and I know that you can't wear them at school, but during the holidays, or at the weekend maybe . . .' Roberto explained, waiting to see her response.

Zoe closed the box and threw her arms around him. The stars jingled around in their box like little bells. Zoe and Roberto stood there for a moment, hugging each other.

'Thank you,' she said to him. 'They're beautiful.' There

was something she was burning to ask him. She plucked up the courage. 'Roberto . . . You know, I kind of thought . . . I thought that you liked Haydée.'

There were a lot of things that she didn't add to this, like, 'Was it just my imagination? Was I right and, if so, why did you change your mind? Did you ask her to go out with you and did she say no? If that's what happened, does it mean that I was just your second choice?'

Zoe didn't know whether Roberto had sensed any of these unasked questions. He just simply said, 'Haydée's pretty and she's nice too. But I like you.'

Zoe smiled in the dark. 'I like you too,' she said to him, and they didn't say another word about it. They said goodbye by squeezing each other's hands really tightly, just for a second, before letting go. And then Roberto kissed her lightly on the lips.

'Did you have fun?' Sara asked her at the dinner table, later.

'Yes, it was great,' Zoe said.

'What pretty earrings. A present?' asked her mum.

Zoe had tried them on, nervously, in front of the mirror. She really loved them. 'Yes, a present,' she answered.

She didn't say anything else. Sara gave her a look and seemed to be about to say something, but then she just bit her lip and drank some water.

They talked about other things, including the animated film that Maria had gone to see with Mum, Dad and a friend from school. Zoe was relieved that the attention wasn't all on her. Afterwards, under the bedcovers, with her earrings removed and carefully put back in their box, she thought about what a special day it had been. If only every birthday could be like that.

'Happy Christmas! Happy Christmas!'

As Zoe walked down the corridors of the Academy, everyone was throwing the words around like confetti, almost without looking to see who they were throwing them at. It could mean only one thing, the Christmas holiday was about to begin. Everyone was really happy because it had been such hard work this term, and now that the days were short too, they all felt more tired than usual. All of the students were in need of a long, relaxing break.

In class, Madame Olenska gave them a short speech.

'Students,' she began.

A faint murmur ran around the room. What's that? Had she stopped calling them 'children' now as well?

'You've worked quite well so far this year,' she continued.

What was this? A Christmas present?

'But of course we're only just a third of the way through the school year and I expect a lot more from you. That's because I'm not going to be here from

February to April. I'm going back to Russia to visit my family.'

Family? Was it possible that the dreaded Madame Olenska had a family?

'So you're going to have a substitute teacher. I want my replacement to have a positive impression of you, so that you'll be able to gain the maximum benefit from working together. I can't tell you who it is yet, but I want you to know that this person is brilliantly talented, and that it's a great honour for the Academy to have this person here as a teacher, even for such a short period. So, now I've told you that, I'd like to wish you a good, relaxing holiday that will allow you to concentrate on the work that will be awaiting you upon your return.'

Madame Olenska emphasised that this was the end of her speech by banging her stick on the floor and making everyone jump, because they were all standing there open-mouthed. The news had taken them completely by surprise. Madame was leaving? How was that even possible, even for a short time? Who would her mysterious replacement be? Would it be a man or a woman? The news had certainly given them a lot to talk about during break-time and in the changing room after class.

There was an atmosphere of anticipation, bubbling over, bright and cheerful, and it must have had more of an effect than Zoe realised, because Zoe saw Madame Olenska in the corridor and before she even knew how it had happened, she had walked up to her and said, 'I'm going to miss you.'

She really meant it. Madame Olenska raised her eyebrows, flashed her very blue eyes at Zoe and said, 'I'll be back soon.' That was it. But that covered it, Zoe thought.

Their last lesson with Kai was fantastic. They tried out a medieval dance – one of those with all the bowing and curtseying and the changing of partners. The music was sweet, solemn and a little bit sad, based around just one flute with a background of *pizzicato* arpeggios made by an instrument that Zoe didn't recognise. The tune was predictable and the steps were regular. You just had to make sure that you didn't make a mess of it, because the dance as a whole was complicated, as everyone was taking part in it, including Kai. There were sixteen of them altogether. There had to be an even number of people in the dance, otherwise someone would have been left out.

Zoe liked the gentleness of the movements. The steps weren't at all complicated, because you didn't have to turn your toes outwards, as you did in classical dance, but walk and run in a natural way instead. However, the arm movements were very important, and so was the posture and position of the neck and shoulders. The top half of the body had to be very expressive and the face had to show the carefree joy of a young person at a spring dance.

When it was Zoe's turn to touch Roberto's arm, she felt

a little thrill and he held her for a moment too long before letting her move on to a new partner, but the exchange was enough to give her face an expression of genuine pleasure. She danced past Laila and recognised the forced smile on Laila's face. Laila didn't like character dance, and made no secret of it. She only managed to do it well because of her incredible self-discipline. Lucas, on the other hand, was having great fun, and his bows were really elegant. Zoe thought about how strange it would have looked to have a black boy at a dance in the Middle Ages. Perhaps he would have been a young prince from exotic lands who had come to explore new worlds.

As the music came to an end, they found themselves facing each other in two rows. Some of the taller girls like Leda had danced the parts for boys, because there weren't enough boys in the class. They seemed to have enjoyed the change in roles. They made a final bow to say farewell. Zoe imagined that in the real Middle Ages, the girls would return to the watchful care of their nurses, and the boys would huddle together with their friends to talk about the beauty and grace of their dance partners. But, of course, that wasn't what happened now. Kai turned off the CD player and started to applaud, with loud, slow claps.

'That was very good,' he said. 'I'm really proud of you. We've known each other for only a couple of months, but I think that we understand each other already. We're working well. We'll put together a fantastic recital piece for the end of the year. We'll start working on it right after the holidays. Until then, relax and have fun. You've really earned it.'

This speech was greeted by spontaneous applause, which was obviously much louder than Kai's clapping, as there were fifteen of them and only one of him. It was a great way to say thanks to a teacher. Zoe had only ever seen this class clapping so enthusiastically when some important dancer was visiting the school as a guest artiste or to teach a specialist course. She clapped and clapped, because every minute of dancing with Kai really was a joy. She grinned to herself as they passed in front of the teacher, one by one, and he said goodbye to them with a smile for each of them.

The only person she'd ever known with a similar name was the boy called Kay who was the main character the Hans Christian Andersen story, *The Snow Queen*, which had actually frightened her a bit when she was small. That Kay was a boy who ended up with splinters of an evil magic mirror in one of his eyes and in his heart, and he fell victim to a spell that forced him to follow the Snow Queen into her frozen realm, where there was no place for feelings. There was only a happy ending to the story because his friend Gerda went on an incredible journey to find him, going through all kinds of danger and finally rescuing him by crying warm tears on him.

So, it was a very sad story. How very different this Kai was! He really wanted them to express their emotions and he demonstrated his own emotions first, by doing the exercises and acting out the dances himself. Character dance was so wonderful, Zoe thought. Really, really brilliant.

CHAPTER NINE

Clearing the Air

'Thanks for the other day. When you dragged Lucas away, I mean,' Zoe said later.

'Oh, don't mention it. I'd have done the same for anyone. What I mean is, I hope you'd do the same for me if I ever needed you to. If I wanted to be on my own with Leo, for example.'

Leo again. Leda was obsessed. He was all she ever talked about. She said he was really funny, but Zoe didn't think he was. Telling a load of jokes, most of them corny old ones, didn't make someone funny, and he did mean impressions of the teachers and sometimes of some of the less popular students, like Jennifer in the second year, who was a bit shy and wore glasses and had to put in contact lenses when she had dance class. Zoe didn't know how to tell Leda what she thought of Leo, because Leda didn't want to hear anything from anyone else. Zoe hoped that she didn't talk too much about Roberto. She had tried not to.

'Our names start with the same letter too,' Leda was saying. 'That's such a weird coincidence, isn't it? It must be fate.'

So, when Leda suggested that the four of them (Leda and Leo, Zoe and Roberto) should go out together on the last Saturday before the Christmas holidays, Zoe said no.

'Have you got something better to do? Or do the two of you want to be alone?' said Leda, in a spiteful tone of voice that Zoe didn't like at all.

They were in Leda's bedroom, in an ocean of pink: pink cushions, pink bedclothes, pink picture frames. Zoe had come home with Leda after school and was staying for dinner.

'No, it's not that. It's just that I don't really want to go out as a foursome, as if we're engaged or something,' Zoe said.

'There were four of us when we went out for your birthday.'

'Yes, but that was different. You and Lucas are my friends and you're friends with each other too. And, to be perfectly honest . . . I don't really like Leo.'

There, she'd said it. Leda just stared at her, with a

cross look on her face.

'I knew it! I just knew you didn't like him,' she said, after a long and icy silence.

Of course you knew, thought Zoe. *You'd have to be blind, deaf and a bit daft not to have spotted it.*

'There's nothing I can do about it,' she said after a while. 'He's not . . . he's just not my type, that's all. He's always talking about himself. He's not interested in anyone else.'

'He's interested in me,' Leda protested. 'He showed me his collection of antique lead soldiers and he told me about his grandmother's place in the country where they go on holiday every summer. He says it's practically a castle.'

Yes, exactly, thought Zoe. She could almost hear him: me, me, me. But she didn't actually say that out loud. Instead, she changed the subject.

'Leda,' she started, in a determined voice. 'It can happen that two friends have different opinions about something. Being friends doesn't mean that we have to think the same about everything, does it? At the moment, we don't seem to be interested in the same things, not even in the same people. But I don't want anything between the two of us to change. I don't know if that's possible. It depends on both of us, I think. I'd like us to carry on doing the things we enjoy together.'

It was a long speech and a difficult one. When she'd finished, Zoe's heart was beating really fast and she was out of breath, as if she'd just run a race. Leda, who was sitting on the bed, hugging a white lace heart-shaped cushion, looked Zoe up and down.

'You sound just like a teacher,' she said. 'A teacher who's trying to teach me something. Giving me a lecture. I don't want you giving me lectures. You're not a teacher. And you're not my mum.'

'You're right,' said Zoe, trying to keep calm. 'I'm not a teacher and I'm not your mum. I'm just trying to be your friend, the way I always have been. Without anyone else getting in the way.'

'But other people are always going to get in the way, aren't they?' Leda protested. 'You can't stop me from seeing Paula or Sophie or . . .'

'But you always say that you get really bored when you're with them.'

'Oh, you know, it's a bit dull sometimes, but we do have some fun. But you, you're always so . . . Oh, I don't know what you are. You're always so sure about what's right and what's wrong. Sometimes you can be really annoying.'

Annoying? What a nasty thing for someone to say. Zoe was about to respond, when Leda's mum knocked on the half-closed bedroom door and, without opening it, said, 'Girls, dinner's ready – are you coming?'

They followed her into the kitchen, not looking at each other. A rectangular pizza was steaming on a baking tray.

It was Leda's mum's speciality. She'd just divided it into three when the phone rang. Leda leaped to her feet. 'It's for me,' she said, and she disappeared into the hallway.

'Go on, Zoe, you just start. Otherwise the pizza will go cold and that'd be a shame,' Leda's mum said. She took a good look at Zoe's face. 'What's up?' she asked. 'Is something wrong?'

'No, no, I'm fine,' Zoe answered. She didn't mean to say anything else, but then the words just slipped out. 'It's just that Leda and I aren't really getting on very well at the moment, and it's making me a bit upset.'

Leda's mum smiled sadly at Zoe. 'It's not just you, Zoe,' she said. 'Leda's growing up and she's changing. She really misses her dad. Sometimes she wants to rebel and she acts as though she doesn't love me any more. I'm sorry, I shouldn't really be saying these things to you, but I know you love her too.

'I'm starting to understand that's the way it is when you have children. You can't always expect them to be how you'd like them to be. I suppose it's the same with friends. We both want Leda to be the way she used to be two or three years ago. But since that's not possible, we're going to have to love the Leda we've got. Well, I am, at least. You don't have to. You can find other friends. But I'd be sorry if Leda lost you as a friend. You're a great girl, Zoe. You've got a strong character, you have your own ideas and you're determined. You're exactly the kind of friend Leda needs. Think about it.'

Leda's mum stopped talking just in time. Leda had hung up the phone and flopped back down on to her chair.

'It was Dad,' she said. 'He said I can stay with him for three days in the holidays.'

'Yes, I know,' her mum said. 'Between Christmas and New Year. Then when you get back, the two of us can go skiing. Okay?'

'I don't think I like skiing any more,' said Leda, pouting like a little girl. 'It's too cold and last year's ski-suit won't fit me now.'

'You can try it on first and then we can see if we need to get you a new one,' Leda's mum said patiently. 'Now are we going to eat this pizza before it turns into rubber?'

Later, as Zoe waited in Leda's room for her dad to come and collect her, there was a strange atmosphere.

'Hey, Zoe,' Leda said, looking out of the window with her back to Zoe. 'I thought about what you said. I was thinking about how I can't help liking Leo. It's like Roberto for you, isn't it? You can't help it. Then I thought about when we were little and we used to do everything together. Do you remember? We used to go and buy clothes together and we played together every afternoon after school and if we didn't see each other on Saturday, then we'd see each other on Sunday.'

Zoe smiled at the memory. 'They used to call us "the twins",' she said.

'That's right. That was before I started growing. No one would think we were twins now, would they?'

'I suppose not,' Zoe agreed.

'But that doesn't matter. I don't mind that we're not so similar now. I still need you, Zoe. Even to give me a telling-off, like you did this evening. I said some really mean things to you and I'm sorry. That stuff about you being a teacher, about lecturing me. It's just that you always seem to be the one who knows the right things to say and to do. I make more of a mess of things. I get confused.'

'But I'm not trying to give you any lessons. We've got Madame Olenska for that and she's more than enough, isn't she?' Zoe said softly.

The two of them smiled at the thought of their teacher. She still seemed to be close to them, even when they were away from school.

'Anyway,' Zoe continued, 'it's not true that I always know what to say and what to do. Sometimes I feel confused too.'

'Maybe we're not all that different really. Even if I am turning into a super-sized ballerina and you're perfectly petite. Even if I do make a fool of myself with boys and you don't,' Leda said, a bit anxiously.

Then, Leda gave a solemn bow, like a court jester that had escaped from their medieval dance class, and the two girls collapsed into giggles. For a moment it felt as though they were still the twins, just like when they were little.

In the car, Zoe asked her dad, 'Do you still see any of your friends from when you were younger?'

'Just the one,' Dad answered. 'Nick. You know, the one who's in advertising.'

'Oh, yes,' said Zoe.

Sometimes Dad pointed at an advert on TV and said, 'My friend Nick made that one.'

'And have you always kept in touch, ever since you were young? Or did you lose touch and then get back together again?' Zoe asked him.

'No, we've always kept in touch with each other. Even though we took different paths at a certain point, we've always managed to meet up every now and then. Sometimes more often, sometimes less often, but we've always got together somehow.'

'And what was it that kept you friends all that time?'

Her dad thought for a while before answering. 'Oh, it was a combination of lots of things, I think. We had some really good times together when we were boys. So, there are the memories. And a sense of respect. But it was mainly the fact that we're so fond of each other.'

'So do you see each other often now?'

'You know, once every two or three months, for lunch. He comes over and meets me from work or I go over to his. We spend a couple of hours together.'

'And what do you talk about?'

'About us. About what we want, about what we've been up to. I tell him all about you lot and he tells me that I'm a boring old family man. But I think he's actually a little envious – he's still on his own. He says that he's looking for his soul mate, but that he still hasn't found the right person.'

'So the two of you are really different.'

'Oh, yes. But you don't need to be the same to be good friends.'

CHAPTER TEN

Marzipan Pigs

Zoe wasn't at all sure about this New Year business. What really was the difference between thirty-first of December and the first of January? The weather was equally cold on both days and they were both as short as each other. It wasn't as if everything changed because it was a new year. In fact, nothing changed. Just the same as when people didn't change and become different on their birthdays.

The holidays seemed to go on for ever, and Zoe knew why. Leda had gone on a skiing holiday with her mum. Roberto was in Milan, visiting his grandparents. Lucas was obsessed with his new Playstation – his number one Christmas present which he'd received after lots of heavy hints, and no one could tear him away from. He'd invited Zoe over to his house to play on it, but she was no good, so he'd got bored after a while and started playing by himself and pretending that he was showing her how to do it.

After a quarter of an hour, bored to death, Zoe took refuge in the kitchen, and made some biscuits with his mum, and he didn't even notice.

'Are you going already?' he'd asked her, when she went into the living room to say goodbye over an hour later, dressed in her outdoor clothes. No, Lucas definitely hadn't been very good company recently.

So Zoe, who was lying stretched out on her bed, was bored. She discovered that boredom, that indefinable mixture of nothingness, laziness and exhaustion, was actually full of things, full of thoughts. For example, she'd just had her birthday, and it had been really nice, with the tea and the presents and Roberto's surprise – the earrings that were now dangling from her ears and swinging along with every one of her movements.

But perhaps the time they went to the exhibition together had been even better, because it was the first time they'd spent any time together. Maybe people should celebrate really special moments in the same way as they normally did with birthdays – a cake, songs and applause, happy faces all around. You could pop into the best cake shop in town and buy something beautiful and delicious, then rush home with it and tell your amazed family, 'I've got something special that I want to celebrate, that's all.'

Or maybe not. Maybe certain important moments weren't meant to be shared or explained. If other people got involved, it might spoil the moment, dilute it somehow. Zoe found it all rather confusing. What was the right thing to do? Maybe there was no right or wrong choice. Things changed all the time. Everything was so complicated, especially when feelings were involved, the things she felt, the people she had feelings for . . .

Zoe reached over to the bedside table, where a pink marzipan pig held a small gold coin in his trotters and stared at her with sugar eyes from inside see-through wrapping. She picked him up. The wrapping crackled. It was a present from her gran. Gran always bought Zoe and her sisters a little marzipan pig at that time of year, because she said that pigs were lucky at New Year.

Zoe was supposed to eat it, obviously, but she couldn't decide how to go about it. It struck her as a bit weird, eating a marzipan pig. If she started at the head, it made her feel like some kind of cannibal. If she started with the feet, it made her feel like a scavenging hyena. Should she bite its throat? At least it would all be over quickly then.

Maria pushed open the door and came in. She was wearing a pink sweatshirt with a horrible sexy doll on the front that Father Christmas had brought for her. Well, it was actually from their Aunty Poppy, who always spoiled

Maria rotten and bought her whatever she wanted. Maria slid over to Zoe's bed, skating on her worn-out anti-slip socks. She sat down on the edge of the bed.

'I ate mine ages ago,' Maria said, and watched her sister dangling the packet between her thumb and forefinger.

'It's pretty strange, isn't it?' Zoe said, thinking aloud. 'Wouldn't it work with fruit instead? I don't know – a pomegranate, or maybe an apple or an orange. I keep thinking that I'm going to hurt the pig if I bite him.'

'But it's not real, silly,' Maria said in the pretend grown-up voice that she'd been trying out recently.

'Do you want it?' Zoe asked.

Maria's face lit up, but then it fell. 'That means that you'll be giving me your share of the good luck.'

'Don't worry about it. I can do without it. How about you eat the pig and give me the coin? Maybe that'll be enough to give me good luck. What do you think?' Zoe grinned at her sister.

It was a deal. Maria bounced out of the room. Five minutes later, she came back, with her mouth full and the gold coin in her hand.

'Here you are,' she said to Zoe, and she dropped the coin on to her tummy. Then she left.

Zoe picked it up. It was a cardboard disc with a four-leaf clover on one side and the number one on the other.

'What are you doing? Counting your treasure?'

That was the thing about her family, Zoe thought –

you hardly ever had a moment of peace. It was Sara this time. She had her hair up in an elegant Japanese bun that she'd fixed with a pencil – something that Zoe had tried to imitate, but without any success. The style emphasised the delicate oval of Sara's face and her long neck. Sara always managed to look great.

'Have you eaten Gran's pig yet?' Zoe asked her, patting the bed to invite Sara to sit down beside her.

Sara sat down and said, 'Of course I have. I love marzipan.'

'I gave mine to Maria.'

'Ah, so that's what she was eating . She wouldn't tell me what it was. Well, it was a very brave thing to do considering Gran always says the pig will bring you luck. That shows real character.'

She ruffled Zoe's hair as if she were patting a dog. They'd never had a dog, much to Zoe's disappointment. But that was no reason for Zoe to stand in as a pet, so she pulled her head away.

'Okay. Message received. You're not a little girl, so I shouldn't treat you like one. You're still my little sister, though. Well, I suppose you're my big little sister, aren't you? Is that okay?'

Zoe nodded. Then she asked Sara, 'What are you doing at home?'

Sara had been spending most of her time lately round at her boyfriend Stephen's house. Nearly every afternoon, in fact, so it was a fair question.

'Oh, I just wanted to see how I'd get on without Stephen, see if I got bored, see if I could handle it. It's sort of an experiment.'

'Is it working? The experiment, I mean. Are you bored or are you managing to cope?'

'I'm not sure. I'm so used to being with him that I feel a bit lost by myself. But I'm doing okay. I'd forgotten how nice it could be just hanging around and doing absolutely nothing.'

She fell back on to the bed, reached out her arms and folded them behind her head.

'Sometimes you need a bit of time to yourself to be able to see things in the right perspective. To see what's important and what's not important. That said, I've not actually had any major revelations so far. I've just spent a lot of time looking at the ceiling. No revelations, no visions, no nothing. But it's really nice spending a bit of time with you. We haven't really spoken to each other for a while, have we? You're always so busy, with your friends and Roberto. He's important to you, isn't he?' Sara paused for breath.

'I think so,' said Zoe. 'It's still all so new.'

'Oh, I know. The first date's wonderful. And it's really wonderful after the first date too!' Sara smiled, a little secret smile to herself.

'But it's not as though you've had a thousand boyfriends, is it?' Zoe pointed out.

'No. But I just wanted to say that it's really wonderful at the beginning, but that it stays wonderful afterwards too. If you love someone, you never get tired of them. It's always a surprise,' she said, sounding very serious and wise as she examined Zoe with her incredibly blue eyes.

'But now you've decided that you want to be on your own,' Zoe pointed out.

'Yes, but you know it's just for today, don't you? He was watching a football match with his mates, and that really isn't my idea of fun. I'd have been bored to death. So I took the chance to do my experiment. No results as yet. I think I'm going to go on spending as much time as possible with him.'

Zoe wanted to spend all of her time with Roberto too. They were lucky that they went to school together, and were even in the same class. Yesterday he had sent her a really sweet text message. *Mi sento solo a Milano. Mi manchi.* Zoe had needed to look up a translation on the internet. Milan was lonely and he missed her. Why was it that some things sounded so much better in Italian?

'Hey . . .' Zoe said to Sara after a long silence. 'Once you said to me that I should make myself interesting if I wanted boys to like me. I didn't do anything, because I didn't know what to do, I had no idea where to begin. I felt like a complete disaster – the clothes I wear, the things I say, the things I don't say . . . I hardly ever say anything when we're all in a group. I feel like I'm all on my own and I can't make anyone notice me. But Roberto still noticed me all the same. So how does that work? Does it mean that he likes me even if I'm not interesting? And why does he like me?'

'You know,' said Sara, studying her nails. 'Sometimes I come out with a load of rubbish. You really shouldn't believe me all the time. Or listen to me. Sometimes I just talk for the sake of it.'

'Oh,' said Zoe, a little disappointed.

'And anyway, you *are* interesting. I'm not just saying that because you're my sister. You're lovely. You've got a great personality. You never do what everyone else is doing just because everyone else is doing it. You use your head. You make your own choices. You're not a chatterbox, but everyone knows that you think a lot. All of that makes you really interesting. Even your shyness is interesting, because it seems as though you have secrets that you don't want to share with other people. Maybe someone might feel the need to find out exactly what those secrets are.'

Zoe could feel herself going red. She was really thrilled. Sara had never paid her such a long and direct compliment ever before. She usually criticised her. But, for the first time, everything she'd said had been nice.

Zoe held out her hand and placed her palm on Sara's forehead. 'Are you sure you're feeling okay?'

Sara lifted Zoe's hand from her forehead and laughed. 'I'm fine, big little sister. I was just saying what I think.

We are a most exceptional family. We're just going to have to wait and see what becomes of that little monkey Maria, but I think it'll be worth waiting for.'

As if she knew that her name had been mentioned, Maria skated back in on her slippery socks.

'I'm bored in my bedroom. I hate my dolls. I'm no good at playing by myself. What were you two talking about?' she whined.

'Secrets, secrets,' Sara said. 'Things for big girls.'

'I'm going to be big one day too,' said Maria, with conviction. 'Big. Like you. First I'll be as big as Zoe, then I'll be as big as you. I'm going to catch up with you.'

'But we're always going to be just that bit bigger,' said Sara. 'That's life, kid.'

Maria looked at her with confusion on her face. But then she took a run-up and threw herself on to the bed, landing in the space between the two sisters.

'Can I have a cuddle with you two?'

'Of course you can,' Zoe said, giving her a big hug.

It was nice, Zoe thought, having a cuddle with her sisters. One of those cuddles where no one was sure exactly who was doing the cuddling and who was being cuddled.

CHAPTER ELEVEN

Saturday Night

On the last Saturday before she went back to school, Zoe always felt there was a special atmosphere. She had to say farewell to those long, timeless days of the holidays, when she could do whatever she wanted to, including staying up late and watching the whole of a film on TV. When she was at school, she only got to see the first part at most and then she had to make do with the descriptions of the rest of the film from her more fortunate friends – ones whose parents didn't pay quite so much attention to the clock and to how much sleep their children had.

Zoe's dad was at work, finishing off something urgent, her mum was lying on their bed, reading a book that she wanted to finish and the three sisters were zapping through the channels, all grabbing at the remote and shouting out their own preferences. There wasn't much on – the usual Saturday evening light entertainment stuff that nobody was interested in, a thriller that didn't seem very thrilling, and a film that was set at the New York City Ballet.

Sara rolled her eyes. 'Oh no, that's all we need. Wouldn't you prefer a nice romance, Zoe?'

'Well, actually, no,' said Zoe, who was a bit curious about the film.

There were no big names in the cast, but she could tell from the trailer that the film really had been made at the New York City Ballet, or at least she recognised the outside of the building. It might be better than the usual Saturday evening kind of thing.

Maria grumbled a bit and then came up with her own suggestion: 'Why don't we watch *Ice Age* again?'

It would have been something like the fourteenth time, so Sara and Zoe's answer was unanimous, 'No!'

'Fine. Well, I'm going to take my books to Mum,' sulked Maria, obviously intending to pester their mum into reading them to her.

Sara and Zoe were left alone. Sara sighed and then said, 'Fine, you win. There's nothing else on anyway,' and she pressed a button on the remote. The ballet film had just started.

It turned out to be pretty disappointing. There was

all the usual stuff that Zoe could have predicted in that kind of film: the girl from the countryside who got a place at the school almost by a miracle, but then had to work four times harder than everyone else to keep up; the brilliantly gifted student who turned out to be a kind of robot programmed for success by her mother; the tyrannical choreographer who felt sidelined by a talented younger choreographer from the other side of the world.

The choreography was so-so, as were the dancers. Zoe watched it all the way to the end, glancing occasionally at her sister, who sank deeper and deeper into the cushions and finally surrendered to sleep. Zoe turned off the television and gave Sara a nudge, but there was no reaction – Sara was in the land of dreams. So Zoe threw a blanket over her, turned the light off and left her there. Mum or Dad would make sure that Sara went to bed when they were locking up and turning things off for the night.

Zoe brushed her teeth and then headed into her bedroom. Something was vibrating beneath her skin, a strange kind of euphoria that she couldn't explain. She got undressed and tried to arrange her clothes in a tidyish pile on her chair, folding up her sweatshirt and, unusually, her jeans as well. Then, instead of putting on her pyjamas, she opened the wardrobe and took out her schoolbag, which was already packed with clean, new things so that she would start the new term properly. Her leotard was neatly folded and, when she picked it up, it smelled of fabric softener. She slipped it on, pulling it up over her bare legs. Her feet were bare too.

How strange. It was the first time Zoe had ever wanted to practise at home. What they did at school was usually more than enough for her. Practising in front of the mirror at home wasn't very comfortable either, as there was no barre and she couldn't really see what she was doing. But still, she was overcome by the need to do practise now.

She opened the wardrobe door and adjusted it so that she could get the best view of what she was doing in the mirror on it, put her feet in first position and started a series of *pliés*. They were the bending exercises that she did at the beginning of every lesson, the ones that reminded her feet and legs and all of her muscles to obey. They were basic exercises, but absolutely essential.

Zoe looked at herself in the mirror. She'd been doing that quite often lately, but this time she didn't check her hair or lip-gloss. This time she was looking at her body, and she liked what she saw.

It was a slim and strong body, compliant and flexible, shaped by exercise and hard work and trained to obey her. It wanted to obey her. Even after a break of two weeks, it was easy for her to return to the positions that seemed so artificial and forced in everyday life, but which were absolutely natural and necessary within the world of dance. Her feet were turned outwards, ready to move apart and cross over. First, second, third, fourth, fifth position: a fluid, gentle series of moves. Her arms moved into the corresponding positions to accompany her legs. The shoulders low, hands graceful and precise. The back perfectly straight, and the head, after she'd inspected the sequence of moves, held high.

Zoe watched her other self in the mirror, the friend that she talked to so often, the one she confided in. They weren't always the same person, Zoe thought, even if they seemed like it. The flesh-and-blood Zoe had another life, other desires, other thoughts. The Zoe in the mirror was a ballerina and she thought about only one thing: being the best ballerina she could be.

'Bye for now,' they whispered to each other. A nod to say goodbye, and the moment vanished as quickly as it had come. Zoe slipped off her leotard, folded it up and put it back inside the bag in the wardrobe.

Five minutes later, her mum came into her room. She must have started doing her rounds. 'Are you asleep?'

'Not yet. Did you manage to get Sara to bed?'

'It was a bit of a struggle. Maria's fallen asleep in my bed, and I don't know if I can manage to move her. She's so long and wriggly that it's like trying to pick up a baby horse. Your dad can move her when he gets in.'

'Can I come into the big bed too?' Zoe blurted out.

'Yes, come on,' her mum said. 'I was thinking of reading

for a bit longer. Why don't you bring a book as well?'

They read for a while, separated by the warm lump of Maria's body.

Then her mum put down her book and said, 'Isn't it such an effort to start again after the holidays? I could do with two more weeks of holiday.'

'Oh, not me,' Zoe said, almost without thinking. 'What I mean is, the holidays are always good fun. But I'm happy to be going back to school.'

'That's so nice,' her mum said. 'Not everyone feels that way, you know.'

'I know,' Zoe said. 'Thanks, Mum.'

'What for?'

'Because I'm doing what I like doing. Maybe I wouldn't have found out by myself that it's what I like doing.'

Her mum smiled and gazed into space for a moment.

'When you started dancing you were such a tiny little thing. It seemed so strange to me, imposing all that discipline on you, all those sacrifices. Sometimes I thought that it was too much for you. But you've really thrown yourself into it with so much passion. Promise me that if you ever have any doubts about what you're doing you'll tell me.'

'I promise, Mum,' said Zoe.

She stroked her mum's foot with her own. And then they both went back to their books.

Ballet Academy

Join in at:

★   ★

piccadillypress.co.uk/
balletacademy   ★

★

Discover more about:
★ the books
★ the dancing
★the Academy
★ and lots more!